Market Town Stories

Tales from Towcester, its hinterland
and a few other places too

Geoffrey Iley

First published in 2022 by Paragon Publishing Ltd.

Copyright © Geoffrey Iley

Cover: Watling Street Galleries

ISBN 978-1-78222-970-4

Book design, layout and production management by Into Print
www.intoprint.net
+44 (0)1604 832149

Dedicated to all writers of all abilities who are looking to improve their skills by trying new things.

Acknowledgements

Illustrations on the front and back are restored images
from an old postcard of both Towcester High Street
and Towcester Town Hall provided courtesy of

Watling Street Galleries
116 Watling Street East
Towcester, Northants
NN12 6BT

www.picture-shop.co.uk

CONTENTS

About the Author

Geoffrey has been writing since childhood but his working life was in the manufacturing industry.
He began to write more seriously in retirement and has published a novel, *Navegator* and a memoir, *A Schoolboy's Wartime Letters*. He lives in Towcester, where he has served as Town councillor and Mayor.

A Midsummer Murder

Gavin Ellis was on the run. He hurtled up the M1 astride his awesome black Ducati motorcycle, weaving through the Saturday traffic, enjoying the adrenaline rush from his Kamikaze moves. He was seriously scared and this stupid, blindly suicidal style of riding suited his mood.

What a fool he'd been. What an idiot to think that he could cheat his crack supplier out of a cool 20K — and then try to get the money to pay him back from a high stakes poker game in Hackney. Well, two games actually, because he had the insane idea that he could somehow win back his first night's losses. So, he'd gone for a second session with the same group of hard-nosed cheats. Now he was owing a massive 100K – and some very nasty characters wanted their money. Those people had very short fuses and they'd sent the notorious Serbian twins, Dragan and Mudrac to collect.

He had managed to get 24 hours grace after their first visit just two days ago. They had stormed into his flat above the Chinese takeaway, roughed him up pretty badly and trashed the place leaving him paralysed with fear. Gavin had drawn the grubby curtains and shut himself away, trying to think of a way out of the mess.

It was early evening on the Saturday when Dragan and Mudrac came to the Chinese takeaway, dressed for violent business in tight-fitting black motorcycling gear. They dismounted from their fearsome yellow Kawasaki bikes and chained them to a lamppost. Mudrac marched over to the door leading to Gavin's upstairs flat and leaned on the bell. Dragan joined him and hammered on the flimsy plywood panel.

After a few moments they got impatient and shoulder-charged their way in. But they found the flat empty. Gavin's fears had kept him in a state of permanent jitters and he was just making a cup of tea when he heard the Serbians' motorbikes arrive.

He dashed to the bathroom at the back of the apartment and slipped out of the window, then slithered down the roof of a lean-to outbuilding before gliding gently away on his faithful Ducati. He was well away before the twins burst in.

Dragan and Mudrac were enraged by their victim's escape. Their total destruction of Gavin's apartment was punctuated by a volley of Serbian oaths. Then, panting from their exertions, they had a muttered conversation, before stomping downstairs and riding off on the Kawasakis, leaving the shattered door of the apartment wide open. It seemed that they had some idea where Gavin might be headed, as they set off purposefully towards London's North circular.

Meanwhile Gavin was trying to calm down and think of an escape plan. Suddenly he had an idea. When he had been a little kid his Mum had worked as housekeeper to a family who lived on a big farm in Northamptonshire.

When Gavin was about nine his Mum got a job as receptionist in a small hotel in Northampton. As he burned up the miles, details came back to him; they lived with a family called Partington at Manor Farm – but he couldn't remember what the nearest village was called, though the town where his Mum shopped had a funny name – Towcester, that was it.

The traffic on the M1 was bunching up now, with a major intersection coming up, Junction 15A. He took the slip road signposted Northampton and Oxford and instinctively headed West. It was a fine June evening; if he could find a barn to kip for the night, perhaps in the morning his memory would be jogged by spotting a signpost to the village. Then he ought to be able to find the farm too.

If he told the people his history and played his cards right, they might give him some temporary work while he came up with a plan to fix the problems he'd left behind in London. But all that could wait until the morning. Right now he was ravenous. Perhaps he could find food in Towcester.

He cruised gently towards the town centre. It was now around 8 o'clock and there seemed to be a lot of happy people about. He could also hear rock, blues and dixieland coming from pubs on the main street. There were people chatting in the doorways too, with drinks in their hands. Then he saw the *'Midsummer Music'* sign on the front of the handsome Town Hall. On an impulse, he turned gently into the lane leading to the church. Finding a small gateway into the churchyard beyond the main entrance, he dismounted and wheeled his bike behind the tower before parking it in the dark shadow beside a large yew tree; the black Ducati was almost invisible. He stripped off his overalls and walked back to the town centre wearing jeans and a black polo shirt. A hamburger and chips would go down well. A few minutes later, with a pint of beer in one hand and his half-eaten burger in the other, he started to relax. Mingling with the locals, Gavin felt their happy enjoyment of the evening was infectious. He stayed for the whole evening in the main street, before standing with the enthusiastic crowd outside Towcester Mill Brewery, watching the firework display being launched from Bury Mount.

It was a spectacular show; huge starbursts filled the sky, punctuated by fiery rockets and loud explosions. And that is why nobody in the festive crowd heard the gentle 'pop' of the silenced Beretta as Mudrac fired an executioner's bullet into the back of Gavin's head at point blank range.

Dragan and Mudrac caught the lifeless body of their victim and, draping his arms around their shoulders, gently carried Gavin into the churchyard. People in the crowd looked on sympathetically, thinking that someone had taken a few drinks too many.

Finding the keys of the Ducati in Gavin's pocket, Dragan started the bike and rode it gently towards the front of the church, where he parked it near a Ford Mondeo.

He retrieved the electronic tracker that he had fixed underneath the fuel tank on the first day they had visited Gavin at his flat.

He tossed the tiny device to Mudrac. 'What an idiot. Did he really think that we would let him get away? Now let's go and enjoy the rest of the fireworks. Nobody will find our dead friend and the Ducati will be safe until we can get Dragoslav to come and fetch it. Everything will be OK. You see, Mudrac, there's never any crime in a place like this'.

April

It is a sunny morning in early April, soon after Easter. Two people stroll arm in arm near Bury Mount. They pause, looking across the mill stream to the Water Meadows. The larger of the two, a man, suddenly looks down at the ground as his shoulders start to shake. The other, a young woman, puts a comforting arm around him and holds him close. 'Daddy, we both know that today would have been Mum's birthday, but she wouldn't want you to be so sad.'

'How can I do anything else, my darling?' He chokes back the tears and wipes his eyes on the sleeve of his parka. She used to love to come here. It's cruel that the virus took her so soon after Christmas.'

April holds her father even closer. 'Daddy, I'm not going back to Manchester until you're through the worst of this, OK? Come on, let's walk and talk.'

They continue, sauntering long Moat Lane and into the Churchyard. There they find daffodils, crocuses and a profusion of wildflowers carpeting the areas where dappled sunlight tiptoes through the trees.

Birds sing and scavenge for nesting materials. They sit on a bench, close to a thatched cottage beside the gated pathway leading to Watling Street.

She turns to her father. 'Now listen to me, Daddy. We're going to get through this together, you and me. I can work for the agency remotely – I've already cleared that with my boss – so I'll be here for as long as it takes.'

'April, sweetheart, I love having you here, so that would be wonderful. It's just that you deserve better than a wet blanket like me for company.'

'You're talking total rubbish, Daddy. Spring is coming and with the lockdown rules being lifted gradually, things must get better. And then we can properly remember Mum.' She wipes away a tear.

'This was always her favourite time of year. A time of rebirth and revival, as she used to say. Anyway, it's my 21st birthday coming up and we need to plan some kind of a celebration. So, what about that?'

At last, his face manages the faintest shadow of a smile. 'Yes, a time of rebirth and a revival for both of us, I guess. So, you should have a proper birthday celebration. You must still have friends here from your schooldays. And you're right, your Mum, my darling Angela, really loved the Spring. She was overjoyed when you were born on 23rd of this month, which happens to be St George's Day – and Shakespeare's birthday too. You just had to be called April.'

They sit quietly for a moment, taking in the tranquility, the scents, the sounds of the morning. After another hug they get to their feet, then leave the churchyard through the gated doorway. Arm in arm, father and daughter dawdle along the path leading to Watling Street.

❧

TANKA

April comes at last
Daffodils and Crocuses,
Gold and violet,
Proclaim that warmth is coming.
Soon we'll have proper Springtime.

Bells at Christmas

(A Victorian pastiche)

It was Christmas eve in Towcester and all along
Watling Street
Were throngs of happy revellers with Christmas fare
replete.
But one poor shambling figure was not like all the rest,
A hunchbacked ragged pauper, his head sunk to his chest.
But suddenly he straightened up – and Quasimodo's hopes
Were buoyed by the sound of ringing as the bell-ringers
tugged their ropes.
He lumbered past the Market Place and then along
Chantry Lane
Till he stood at the door of St Lawrence Church and felt
he was home again.
True, it wasn't like Notre Dame, but this team clanged
with the best;
Little they knew that the hunchback was about to make
a request.
He beat his fists on the old oak door, *'Ouvrez la porte!'*
he roared,

'I muss get up to ze bell tower for my strength to be restored.
If I miss my daily stint wiz ze bells, I'll wither and waste away –
So, permettez-moi to join you till ze break of Christmas Day.'

The bell-tower captain pondered, then yelled 'Come in; feel free.'

Quasimodo sprang to a bell rope.

'Allez mes braves!', cried he.

Then merry peals from Towcester rang through the Christmas night
And a flurry of gentle snowflakes created a landscape white.
And children as far as Abthorpe
who heard those distant bells
Called out to their doting parents,
'we know what that sound foretells;
Those far-off bells are magical – they'll bring us such soothing rest,
We'll all have a wonderful Christmas and one that is truly blessed.'

* * *

Quasimodo enjoyed his Christmas with our bell-ringers of renown,
Wherever his travels take him, he'll remember our festive town.

Celebration at Lactodorum

This piece was inspired by a very ancient oyster shell, unearthed when digging in the garden of a house in the town. A spade had disturbed the earth lying just below the probable location of the southeast tower of the wall surrounding Lactodorum. This strategically important Roman stronghold would later be known as Towcester.

* * *

This text comes from a parchment found in the ruins of Pompeii. It had been stored in an amphora, so that most of it was protected during the volcanic eruption that destroyed the city.

To my dear brother, Antoninus Marcellus, greetings from the middle part of Brittania, where I have been stationed these last three months with my troop of horse, in command of the garrison here at Lactodorum. We are attached to the XIIIth Legion under the command of Barnatus Murano, a veteran and a fine soldier.

He returned victorious only two hours ago from a mighty battle just a short distance from the town. Now, bathed and arrayed in his finest uniform we are sitting together on the battlements of the south-eastern tower of Lactodorum. Murano rose even further in my estimation during the time we spent together this evening, just the two of us, feasting and toasting his victory. When talking to him on previous occasions, I had judged him to be dull and unintelligent. Tonight was different; I soon realised that he is a brilliant strategist.

Though he is a modest man, our conversation revealed that it was his skill that enabled Suetonius to inflict a crushing defeat on that she-wolf Boadicea and her rabble just before they could reach the town's defences.

Our Governor, Suetonius, had assembled an army of 10,000 to deal with the horde of Iceni and Trinovantes marching north towards us here. They had pillaged and ransacked everywhere along their route, putting many Romans and our allies to the sword.

Our force was greatly outnumbered, but Murano knew the lie of the land very well and Suetonius approved his plan to let Boadicea's undisciplined horde think that we were in full retreat.

Our men, with the XIIIth Legion at the centre, fell back north-westwards up the valley of a river they call the Tove. He chose a place only three miles from here to be the killing ground. On either side there was dense forest and, as the width of clear ground between the trees gradually reduced, so our men ran before them. Then, at the blast of a trumpet, they turned to face the tribesmen where the clear space was at its narrowest, locked their shields and withstood the onslaught. Suetonius' hidden archers filled the air with a storm of arrows, then our cavalry swept out of the forest on either side and cut the barbarians to ribbons.

Soon the Tove ran red with blood of the dead tribesmen, for even their escape to the southeast was barred by another wall of shields. Women and children in their baggage train were not spared, but the slaughter was a just punishment and an example to these barbarous tribes. Boadicea was captured before she could take poison and Suetonius is taking her away to face punishment in Londinium, taking his legions with him. They will need to guard that she-devil well, or she will find a way to take her own life before she tastes Roman justice and the punishment that awaits those who threaten our Empire.

It has been a great privilege to spend time alone with Murano to enjoy our celebration feast together. We had some wild boar, which we both declared the best we had ever tasted, but perhaps the flavour was improved by the great victory today. I must also tell you that we had some magnificent oysters, sent by sea from Colchester to the mouth of a great river called Ouse, then upstream as far as the next small garrison a few miles south of here — then by horseman along the highway to Lactodorum. They arrived perfectly fresh and the two of us stood shoulder to shoulder giving thanks to Mars for the victory, toasting each other in Samian wine and throwing the oyster shells over our shoulders into the darkness. Truly, it was a night to remember...

The document has crumbled to dust at this point, so that the identity of the writer remains unknown despite intensive research.

Crossing The River

There have been crossings here since time began.
When men appeared – and women too
Wading across this ford for berries, nuts and meat.
After an age, they herded sullen livestock through the stream
Seeking new pastures and a place to build.
The people prospered, but the river was a curse.
Sometimes it flooded so that folk could not get home.
Then came the bloodshed. Many lives were lost
as warring tribes
Fought over lands for wealth, prosperity and power.
The Romans put a stop to all of that;
they crushed the locals,
Using new-captured slaves to fashion river crossings.
I'm told a sturdy wooden bridge was built just here,
To bear a Roman *strada* for their marching legions.
But, when those conquerors went, the bridge did not survive
Those dreadful years of darkness; broken to firewood
It went up in flames, like all the ravaged settlements nearby.
After the passage of some centuries came fragile peace.
And then, they say, a dark-skinned man surveyed
the shallows here,
Sighting along a special staff, using the strings and pegs
Peculiar to his craft, with diagrams drawn in sand
Showing his masons what they had to do
To raise his fine stone arches for a major road.

900 years have passed – his brainchild still survives.
The Old Bridge stands, but I'm convinced
it's obsolete today
For massive modern trucks need bigger, stronger bridges.
A clever youngster's newer skills conceive one soaring arch.
For him no staff, no strings and pegs, no drawings
in the sand.
Laser sight lines, electronics, computer printouts,
do the work.
Prefabricated structures are assembled from a kit.
Important people praise the New Bridge
and its graceful form.
But, will it last at least 900 years? Sadly, that's a matter
for debate.
Will man exist so long? One day, I fear
the doom of everything
When radioactive rain makes all things living
obsolescent too.

Abandon Ship

Jock Macfarlane, captain of *MV Excalibur*, rubbed his eyes and looked at the letter again. The envelope had been delivered by courier just before his luxury cruise ship left Brest on the last leg of the voyage, to Southampton. What the hell was the urgency? Well, now he knew; his immediate boss, Foster Benson, director of Operations for Camelot Line, had written to him personally. The letter, a sycophantic, empty set of platitudes said that the proprietor, Arthur King – known in the industry as King Arthur – had decided to sell off his older ships. This would let him embark on a major expansion in river cruises and also build a gigantic floating palace for the Far Eastern market.

The Camelot Line had been built on the foundations of a near-bankrupt ferry company, *Seaspeed*. Arthur King, the new owner, had bought it cheaply and renamed it as a homage to King Arthur and a tribute to his own ego. He was also a bully and a ruthless businessman. He and Jock had been at loggerheads ever since they crossed each other. This was soon after Jock, master of the *North Sea Greyhound* had found himself as part of the assets acquired by this ambitious autocrat. But Arthur King did respect profitability – and there was no doubt that Jock Macfarlane achieved better financial results than anyone else. So, he found himself captain of the flagship *Excalibur* despite a number of angry spats with the autocratic boss of the Camelot Line.

A year or two afterwards Jock's only daughter Mary was killed by a hit and run motorist. Arthur King denied him compassionate leave. His grief-stricken wife Morag took her lonely life three months later. He swore a sacred oath to have his revenge one day and sank into depression for a while, but stayed at his post, becoming obsessed with 'his' ship. He prowled every inch of *Excalibur*, learning every last inch of his floating home. Meanwhile, with nothing to spend his salary on, Jock built up a pile of savings – prudently tucked away in a Swiss bank. His only indulgence was a modest beachside villa near a lovely mediaeval port on the Black Sea and a small run-down yacht moored at Warsash, just beside the Solent.

There was more in that hateful letter; Jock would be offered a shore job as Director of Training. Or, of course, he could take early retirement. In any event, this would be *Excalibur's* last cruise before being sold for rebuilding. He swore loud and long, then tossed the crumpled letter into the waste bin and reached for the computer keyboard. It took no time at all to compose his resignation. He smiled grimly as he poured himself a generous tumbler of Talisker Malt Whisky. During the next hour he planned a spectacular revenge, which involved a lavish retirement party he would give himself the night before they reached Southampton. Soon after that, Arthur King would wish he had never been born.

At 0900 hours on the final day at sea, Jock Macfarlane called a staff meeting. He told his senior officers of his impending departure and the circumstances. There was an immediate uproar, but he eventually restored order. At this stage, he was unable to give them any assurances about their own futures, but he expected clarification in an hour or two. Meanwhile, they must all make a big effort to plan a magnificent leaving and retirement party tonight; they all had much to do and he left the Hotel Manager, Ulrik Svenson, to take charge of the arrangements. Jock closed his notepad and walked out, leaving some very disturbed colleagues with the job of conjuring up an unforgettable celebration.

Svenson was used to organising big functions. Within an hour, he had a plan and information sheets were being distributed to all the passengers' suites. While this was happening, Jock was making arrangements of his own, roaming the ship like a prowling wolf. By now, every member of the crew knew what was going on and members of the crew in every department from garbage disposal to the engine room and kitchens, pumped his hand and wished him well, even though they were in the dark about their own futures. Back in his cabin, Jock had a long and acrimonious phone conversation with his boss. Foster Benson conceded that the short notice was regrettable, but that Arthur King's decision was final and, in any case, he was currently on holiday and not to be disturbed. However, some officers and crew would be reassigned and, as a goodwill gesture, Foster had been authorised to offer all those made redundant 5% more than the minimum statutory redundancy pay. Jock responded with an earful of colourful expletives and slammed the phone down. After making a few private phone calls and emails, he went to the bar and circulated with the passengers, the soul of hospitality and good humour.

Later, after a hasty lunch in his cabin, Jock took his turn at the wheel before returning to his cabin to pack for his departure the next morning and dress for the gala night. Before going to the black-tie reception, he went through the gleaming kitchens, adding a bottle of his own, specially doctored, Balkan firewater to the huge silver vat of Celebration Punch. After that, the festive night passed in a blur. The Punch was a huge success, but Jock warned his colleagues off that concoction – 'it gives a lethal hangover'

– and they all stuck to Champagne. Magnificent food came and kept coming; more wine flowed. There were speeches, with tributes to Jock; then his own, sad farewell, followed by a brilliant Cabaret featuring talented crew members. Finally, there was a rather tipsy rendering of Auld Lang Syne.

Jock went back to his cabin, declining the offer of a nightcap from the senior officers, and lay on his bunk. At 3am his alarm woke him. He was fully prepared for his mission. He made a check on the ship's location. Then he stripped and put on a wetsuit brought earlier from his own secret locker low down, close to the bilges. In that hideaway he had stored equipment from the time of his service in the Royal Marine Commandos. He went back there briefly, keeping a few items in his waterproof rucksack. Before he left and sealed the concealed door behind him, he activated a device he had constructed earlier. Then he slipped like a ghost through the deserted ship. Nobody saw the shadow that slipped into the black moonless waters. Two hours of swimming later, Jock was picking up more kit from the cabin of his boat at Warsash. At 8am his empty cabin was discovered. By that time breakfast was in full swing, though some passengers were feeling unwell and struggling to prepare for disembarkation at around 10 am. By that time there was a full scale alert, but Jock was nowhere to be found. That wasn't surprising, as he had just boarded a Lufthansa flight at Amsterdam after his early morning KLM flight from Southampton. By the time the police began to issue his details, he had changed flights at Frankfurt and was heading east.

A week later Jock was relaxing close to a sandy beach. He was in his own seaside villa, close to the beautiful old port of Baku. He was enjoying a slightly outdated copy of *The Times*, obtained in Khagani Street from the British Embassy where he posed as a tourist. In a few moments he found the headline **'Cruise Ship Passengers affected by norovirus – Arthur King forced to issue apology and promise compensation'**. Those unfortunate passengers had evidently drunk the Celebration Punch. Jock frowned; it was a pity about the collateral damage. He shrugged and a bottle of champagne was quickly opened; its companion would have to wait another week or two.

It was just eighteen days after Jock's arrival in Baku that his daily visit to the Embassy was interrupted by a summons to the Ambassador's office. There, he was shown a despatch from London; all embassies were to report the whereabouts of Jock Macfarlane, former captain of *MV Excalibur*. His disappearance was linked to a norovirus outbreak and to an act of sabotage. A small hole had been blown in the ship's hull by a radio-controlled device in a secret locker below the waterline. *Excalibur* had been *en route* to a Baltic shipyard in Germany for handover to new owners, but was now sunk in the Kiel shipping canal. The report added that costs of repairs and compensation for closure of a major shipping route could be fatal for the Camelot Line.

Jock already knew that he couldn't be extradited from Azerbaijan, but his cup of happiness overflowed when *The Times* reported that Arthur King had been declared bankrupt and was under investigation for fraud. In his villa, the second bottle of champagne was soon being opened by a smiling blonde lady. Revenge, Jock reflected, could be very sweet indeed.

჻

The Christmas Legions
A Victorian Pastiche

This is a Towcester legend, and it's one that's often told
As Christmas Day approaches
and the nights are bleak and cold.
Then Watling Street falls silent; gone is the traffic's hum.
And children hear a murmur, from the beat
of a ghostly drum
As down the Roman highway the phantom legions come.
And as their ghostly sandals
March down the ancient street,
Their spirits sense those children
Who're tidy, clean and neat.
Then, Christmas Day will be a joy
For every virtuous girl and boy.

* * *

But as for those who've not been good –
well, that's a different tale
They won't enjoy their Christmas;
their toys will break and fail.
So, Towcester children, please be good, for if not
you should fear
The march of phantom legions –
and Christmastide is near!

Two Famous Parents

The Old Rectory
Grimscote
Northamptonshire

23rd July 2015

My dear Richard,

It is only a few days since you were here; now you're on the other side of the world, resuming your secondment from the Royal Navy to *HMAS Tasmania*. As you know, I'm very proud that you are keeping up the Gilbert family's long-standing tradition of seamanship. Even so, I could wish that you and the family were nearer just now, instead of being based in Sydney, as I've had some sudden and rather worrying news. The fact is that a routine visit to Doctor Henderson yesterday revealed that I've got something a bit nasty and they're taking me to Northampton General in an hour or so for surgery.

Hopefully, there will be a satisfactory outcome, but it seemed a good idea to drop you a line 'just in case'. Most of my friends have passed away now, so I find myself with only the dogs and my books for company. Truth to tell, it's a bit lonely here since your mother died so suddenly four years ago. Thank heaven for Mrs. Johnson, who keeps the house running like clockwork.

Anyway, we had a good talk about everything during your stay and there's not much else to say now – except for one very important matter. I'll come to that in a moment, but humour me with a digression.

Let's imagine that you were asked to choose two notable people that you could have had as parents, then who would they be? For me, a couple of candidates stand out. For a mother to be proud of, what about Queen Elizabeth I? What a woman! Not only did she succeed in everything; masterminding the defeat of the Spanish Armada and rousing the Nation with a stirring speech that put even the mighty Winston Churchill in the shade; creating a cult of personality that endeared her to every English heart (fervent Catholics accepted, I suppose); and finally dying in office after a truly magnificent reign.

She eclipsed even Boudicca, Maggie Thatcher who didn't last the distance and Queen Victoria who, after Albert's death, actually achieved little in her lengthy reign.

What about a famous father? There are so many to choose from – I don't think we should restrict our choice to actual husband and wife partnerships, but it could be interesting to choose contemporaries. So, what about Sir Francis Drake?

Personally, he wouldn't be my preferred candidate; a bit of a ruffian, somewhat coarse and, if contemporary accounts are to be believed, not really the master tactician who destroyed the Armada. The strategic mistakes made by the Spanish commanders were far more significant.

So, I would select Sir Walter Raleigh, a cultured man from a good family. Among other things he was responsible for popularising tobacco (today we wouldn't think of that as a good thing, but it was enormously significant) and that arose from his establishment of the first colony in North America. Later, he also introduced the potato. Of course others, notably the French, had aspirations there too. But Raleigh's footprint set the path for North America to become important in the worldwide propagation of the English language. As an accomplished writer and poet he would have been proud of that; he was also a successful military man and an accomplished sailor.

So, let me nominate Queen Elizabeth and Sir Walter Raleigh as my 'parents of choice'. But this isn't just a piece of whimsy. It is now time to reveal to you, my dear boy, the Gilbert Family Secret. It is my sacred duty to pass this on to you under an oath of secrecy, while binding you, in turn, to explain it to young Mark – not too soon, but before you depart to a higher place – because it is important for so many reasons.

At last I can get to the point: your far-off ancestor, Raleigh Gilbert, was actually the love child of Queen Elizabeth I and Sir Walter Raleigh. You and I are directly descended from him through the firstborn males of the Gilbert line.

How did this come about? In a way it was very simple. Sir Walter had been heading a very successful campaign in Ireland and returned as a hero to Elizabeth's court.

One day, when the queen wanted to cross a muddy road, Raleigh whipped off his expensive cloak and laid it over a puddle, so that her shoes and skirts should not become dirty. Elizabeth was charmed and invited Sir Walter to join her inner circle.

Other senior courtiers were dismayed, but the queen became obsessed with this charming, cultured young man and a clandestine liaison resulted in the birth of a son. The voluminous robes worn by the queen had concealed her pregnancy; the infant was spirited away in secret and brought up in a west country household, where a wet nurse reared the child. That infant was our ancestor Raleigh; his surrogate mother was none other than Anne Gilbert, wife of Sir Walter Raleigh's half brother, Humphrey.

Following the secret birth, it was important to avoid any possibility of malicious gossip. It was decided that Sir Walter ought to wed and he duly married Elizabeth Throckmorton, one of the queen's ladies in waiting. At the time it was said that The Virgin Queen was furious about the match, but this was a smoke screen which successfully protected the royal secret. In time Raleigh did, in fact, fall out of favour, but the charade lasted long enough to do its work. I should add that all these facts are true; you can verify them if you wish, but I beg you to use the utmost discretion.

Why does this matter, and why the secrecy? Well, apart from the historical interest, it could mean that you, Richard, should be the rightful inheritor of the British Crown. That can of worms is far too awful to contemplate at the moment but the day might come when it is our duty to reveal the Gilbert family's royal lineage. Who knows?

I'm feeling a bit tired now, so I will close with my everlasting love to you, the lovely Julia and those delightful youngsters Mark, David and Emma.

My blessings to you always,

Father

Author's note: This is, of course, a piece of fiction. But the character of Raleigh Gilbert really existed and the timings (almost) work.

࿊

Charlie

My name is Harry Westfield and my brother Charlie is two years younger than me. When our Mum and Dad died in an accident, we were brought up by Nan, our only surviving relative. At that time we were still at primary school but we gradually recovered from that loss in the love and warmth of her home on The Shires in Towcester.

In due course we both went on to secondary education at Sponne School. Here we both did well, but Charlie was the golden one. I was good, but Charlie easily outshone me and was getting top marks in almost every subject. I didn't mind even when he seemed to be blessed with an outgoing personality, attracting more friends and invitations than I ever did. When A levels came around, I got decent grades and after a degree course in Accountancy at Warwick University I landed a job with a big commercial firm in Milton Keynes.

But when Charlie's turn came, he got a whole bunch of A*s, notably in Maths and Spanish. So, it was no surprise when he was awarded a scholarship to read Economics at Cambridge.

Girlfriends came and went. I had met Sarah at Warwick and in due course we were married, living in a rented flat in Towcester beside Waitrose, so that I could be near to Nan. When she passed away from a massive heart attack, the house on the Shires was inherited by Charlie and me. Sarah and I, with our first baby on the way, moved in and settled down to family life.

Meanwhile, Charlie was having the time of his life in London. He had been headhunted by the Spanish bank Santander straight out of Cambridge. With his fluency in Spanish, he climbed the promotion ladder at speed, while despite punishing working hours, his social life was a whirlwind. The two of us kept in constant touch via social media, but Charlie couldn't often get back home. So, we usually had to meet in London to have any face to face contact.

I began to worry about his friends and behaviour– with hindsight, he seemed to be troubled and must have started using drugs.

Then things happened very quickly. Charlie was given a major promotion into the Brazilian arm of Santander and moved to their principal office in Sao Paulo. The messages then became less frequent. It seemed that my brother was getting into the Brazilian music scene and even joined a Samba team in advance of the local Mardi Gras parade. Charlie was able to take some holidays but had to stay close to base because of the country's economic instability. So, a visit back to the UK was out of the question. Then, after almost three years away, he made contact to say that he was coming to a symposium in Oxford in July. A weekend with us would be just like old times. He badly wanted to see me, Sarah and the children – we now had a boy and a girl.

We were thrilled. My charismatic brother was coming to stay and we intended to make a fuss of the prodigal. Charlie had rented a car and planned to drive to Towcester early on Friday evening. We had put the kids to bed and Sarah had got a rib of beef roasting in the oven, when I realised I'd missed a text message from Charlie.

'I need to see you first, Bro, before I come round to the house. Please meet me for a drink around 7 at The Plough.'

I tried an immediate ring back, but the phone was off and I realised that Charlie would already be on his way. With a quick explanation to a frowning Sarah, I drove to the Market Square and sat in the front bar at The Plough, nursing a half of bitter. With the evening sun in my eyes, it was hard to see customers as they came in. So, I was speechless when a lovely blonde woman suddenly materialised on the stool next to mine.

'Hello, Harry', she said, 'What about a big kiss for Charlie, your long-lost sister?'

The Smile

It was the first time that he saw her smile. Will was standing on the doorstep of the handsome house just off Towcester's Northampton Road. His hand still fluttered near the doorbell, his face frozen, speechless. 'Come on in,' she said brightly, 'You must be Will. My name's Jenny. Tom and the others are in the games room and the final's due to start in about ten minutes, I think. Come on through.' She turned and walked down the hallway, trailing not-quite perfume like some magic, invisible cloak. He meekly followed her, stunned by a lightning strike that he hadn't seen coming. After that, Will made all the excuses he could find to visit her house.

Things moved at breakneck speed. After dating for only a few weeks, Will proposed, Jenny accepted and their whirlwind courtship culminated in a fairytale wedding at St Lawrence's.

A honeymoon in the Caribbean was followed by an idyllic time setting up home in a thatched cottage in Stoke Bruerne.

While Jenny continued her career as a physiotherapist, Will got a promotion and soon they started to think seriously about starting a family. A year later and with no signs of a pregnancy, they sought medical help. After weeks of tests, a kind specialist at Northampton General told them that their only hope was a course of IVF treatment; expensive, but the best option. They went ahead, but after three rounds of treatment, the results were a disaster.

Jenny and Will were distraught. Driving home to Stoke Bruerne after another visit to the specialist they started to argue. All those rounds of painful treatment had been unsuccessful, with two ending in miscarriages. What should they do? Will suggested another round of IVF, but Jenny was having none of it. 'It's all very well for you,' she said, 'you're just a man.' She raised her voice. 'You don't have to deal with the pain and the despair if it all goes wrong for a fourth time'.

Will was dismissive. 'You really can't be serious. Surely you're not suggesting adoption. That's just not going to happen. I'm damned if I'll be father to a child that isn't really ours. And that's final!'

The bickering developed into a full-scale argument and by the time their homeward route reached the M1 Junction, Will was really angry and not concentrating on the traffic. Jenny was shouting, 'I just want a baby, any baby', as an oil tanker joined the roundabout from the M1. Will, distracted, saw the danger too late and hit it broadside on. Another car ploughed into theirs and within seconds they were engulfed in a fireball.

Will was trapped and succumbed to his injuries. Later, he was pronounced dead on arrival at A & E. Miraculously, the driver of another car managed to drag Jenny out of the smashed glass of the passenger door. She survived despite a broken leg, a dislocated shoulder and extensive burns. But after the accident, even after she had recovered physically, she would speak to nobody, not a single word. Her desperate parents and her brother Tom looked for help and eventually found a psychological trauma specialist, who agreed to treat her.

He spent many sessions trying unsuccessfully to break Jenny's wall of silence, realising that she blamed herself for

Will's death. But nothing brought any glimmer of light to those dull brown eyes.

Hypnosis failed. Looking at old photographs, even listening to her favourite music got no response. Then, just when the case seemed hopeless, a colleague suggested that film and TV excerpts might be helpful. For the first time since the start of treatment, the ghost of a reaction showed in Jenny's lifeless eyes. Then, on a grey day in February, he showed her a YouTube clip. It was the Evian TV ad that featured a troupe of dancing babies. At last there was the first hint of a smile.

'Of course,' she cried, 'why didn't I think of it sooner? I was blinded by guilt, but this changes everything. I could adopt a baby, one that I can make my own.' And, finally, she laughed.

The Tea Tray

Harry Watson nursed a mug of tea as he looked out of the grimy window at a small drab back yard. So, this dump is what uncle Freddie had left him in his will – and he needed it like a hole in the head. The house had once been Freddie's corner shop at the corner of two terraces in one of Birmingham's industrial districts. But he, Harry, was very well off and newly retired from his job in a merchant bank. But as his uncle's only surviving relative – and sole beneficiary of the old man's will – he had rashly volunteered to wind up the estate. And just look at what he'd taken on; a small balance in a savings account and a semi-derelict piece of Victoriana in a wretched part of this urban sprawl. At least the place was more or less clean and the electric kettle worked.

Harry turned away from the window and glanced in the old mirror above the sink as he washed his mug. He had worn well, with piercing grey eyes, a good head of greying hair and strong features. With above average height, a good physique and a lively mind, some women had found him very attractive – but that sort of attraction was part of his past life. Now it was time to get started on today's task; sorting out piles of Freddie's stuff, collected over a lifetime.

By midday, after two hours of work, he had filled several bin liners with clothes, bed linen and assorted junk. Then he decided to take a break and visited an unattractive local pub for a pint of bitter and an anonymous hotpot. When Harry returned he decided to tackle the cupboard under the stairs. A pile of boxes toppled into the small hallway. Harry selected one at random and carried it to the kitchen table. It contained a stack of old photograph albums and he couldn't resist leafing through them. Soon he saw faces he recognised; uncle Freddie and his wife Hilda who died during the blitz while her husband was at El Alamein; his own parents, Jack and Emma, long dead and gone. Then came a surprise – an image he had never seen before – a laughing group outside a thatched village inn, the White Horse. There stood Freddie with his faithful Standard Vanguard in the background, his arm round the shoulders of a ten-year-old Harry, with his own Mum and Dad alongside.

Harry had to sit down for a moment. He fell into a reverie with the album on his knee. Those were happy days, when the future held such promise. What had his own life become? A sterile search for money and status with nothing to show for all that striving; a failed marriage, no children, a big useless house in Solihull, membership of a snobbish golf club, no real friends. What had been the point of it all? He needed to reclaim the spirit of those times. Taking the picture from the album, he resolved to find that village if it took him months, years even.

The next box held another surprise: under a pile of kitchen junk was an old tea tray with a faded picture of a beautiful bird, a woodpecker perhaps, with flowers and a message in bold lettering reading 'What makes you come ALIVE?' Harry was transfixed. It was another reminder of happier times in the countryside. He picked up the tray and compared it with the view from the dirty window. The message on the tray, with the word 'ALIVE' in capitals, struck home – he certainly wasn't alive now and hadn't felt truly alive for many years. That old photograph, along with the tea tray and its message were powerful signals. He needed to change direction.

* * *

Over the next few weeks Harry scoured the countryside within a fifty-mile radius of Birmingham, searching for that elusive village with the White Horse Inn. Eventually he decided to cast his net wider and finally found a possible location – but he needed to check it for himself. The White Horse at Woolstone, near Swindon was thatched and might have been the inn in the family photograph. One Monday he packed a bag, threw it into the Lexus and set off in the general direction of Swindon, intending to stay for a night or two exploring neighbouring beauty spots. Swindon itself was unappetising, so Harry settled on the small town of Faringdon as his base and checked into the picturesque Old Crown Hotel in the afternoon. The fair-haired woman in charge of Reception smiled a warm welcome. She showed him to a comfortable room with character and stylish traditional décor.

Harry took a nap, waking in time for an early dinner and found that he was one of a handful of diners. A young waitress showed him to a corner table, giving him a menu and wine list, but a few minutes later it was the woman from Reception who came to take his order. He chose traditionally: soup of the day (a delicious oxtail), roast pork with all the trimmings and apple pie with custard to follow. He had a half bottle of Beaujolais to wash it down. When he ordered a brandy to go with his coffee, it was the woman from Reception who brought the balloon glass to his table.

"I don't know if you know the area, sir, but there is a lot to see around here. There's the famous White Horse at

Uffington and the Cotswold Water Park just the other side of Swindon."

"As a matter of fact, I'm heading off to the White Horse Inn in Woolstone tomorrow – that's quite near Uffington, I think. Perhaps I could have lunch there."

"An excellent choice, sir. We've heard very good reports of their food."

Harry watched as her shapely form drifted away, stopping briefly to talk to other diners. He went to bed early, feeling desperately tired, and fell asleep with the television on.

He woke refreshed, skipped breakfast and, as the June morning was fine, drove the Lexus to Wantage for coffee and a croissant, before exploring the hillside near Uffington with its magnificent White Horse carved into the chalk by an ancient people. Lunch at the White Horse Inn at Woolstone was delightful. It was definitely the backdrop for his family snapshot, but the present owners could not suggest a date for the old photograph and had no more information to offer; it had been taken long before their time.

Harry's expedition had been disappointing. He returned to Faringdon and walked around the little town until he found a tearoom. Entering this chintz-and-frills oasis, he was surprised to see the woman from Reception. She was wearing a dark blue two-piece that emphasised her lively blue eyes and fair complexion. She seemed preoccupied and was sitting alone.

"A penny for your thoughts. Do you mind if I join you?"

"Not at all"

"May I ask your name?"

"It's Helen – Helen Patterson."

Harry ordered tea and, after a shaky start, they were soon talking about everything; family, books, holidays. After a while Helen looked at her watch.

"I must get back. Time to get ready for dinner."

"Yes, of course. Please save me the same table as last night. I think it brings me luck."

"Of course."

She flashed a smile and was gone.

Harry had no reason to leave Faringdon so, over the next few days the pattern was repeated; stilted, almost formal, words in the Old Crown Hotel; relaxed, personal conversations in the tearoom.

On Friday, Harry told Helen about his reason for coming to the area; the old photograph, the faded images and words on the tea tray that had jolted him out of his sterile existence. She looked up at him and smiled.

"Harry, that is the most amazing story. Do you think that your journey has been worthwhile?"

He reached across the table and took her hand. She did not pull back and Harry looked into her eyes.

"Oh yes, absolutely. You see, you are the one that makes me come alive."

Flying Visit

The twin-engined Cessna taxied close to the ramshackle terminal building on the perimeter of the dusty airfield. As it came to a bumpy standstill on the cracked taxiway, the passenger door flew open and a tall, rangy man gently eased himself onto the sun-baked concrete. Max Milton, wearing a crumpled lightweight jacket and well-worn jeans, winced as he reached back into the plane and pulled out a battered leather bag and a computer case. He set them down gingerly as he adjusted his Ray-Bans, put on a wide-brimmed hat and waved to the dark-skinned man in a smart tropical suit lounging in the shadow of the building.

'Can you give me a hand with these please? My back's killing me.'

The man languidly waved to a porter with a small barrow, who trundled it over, picked up both bags and escorted Max to the stranger beside the building. He held out his hand and greeted the new arrival in fluent English, with a slight French accent.

'I am Ibrahim Falouni and it is a great pleasure to meet you Mr. Milton. We have been expecting you. Welcome to El Merk (I am sure that you will find your visit memorable.'

'Thanks for coming out to meet me. I had hoped to see Chuck Jorgens here, but I guess he's got his hands full dealing with the emergency.'

Max turned and waved as the pilot taxied the Cessna away for takeoff. Meanwhile, Ibrahim signalled to a Humvee parked in the shade of a palm tree a short distance away. Immediately it drove over to pick up the new arrival and his bags. Within a few minutes Milton was heading away from the airfield, along with Ibrahim and the porter, who sat alongside the driver (a formidable black guy with a shaved head whose muscles amply filled his battle fatigues. As they drove into the desert, Max tried to ask for details of the disaster at the wellhead, but it seemed that the information was sketchy. Even though Ibrahim was a representative of the Algerian Ministry of Energy and Mining he had only just arrived himself and knew very little. So, as the miles rolled by, Max reflected on the situation.

He had picked up the phone call around 10pm the previous day and within twenty minutes he was outside his bachelor apartment, jumping into a taxi to Houston airport. Max Milton, known as "The Professor", was a Brit who had enjoyed a stellar career as a chemical engineer. Headhunted by a huge petroleum engineering conglomerate based in Texas, he had inherited the mantle of the late Red Adair. Wherever in the world there was serious trouble with a well (oil or gas) "The Professor" was the man to fix the problem. Unlike the flamboyant Adair, this quiet, private man rarely used massive explosive charges, preferring to use his unique chemical cocktails, known as 'Milton Suppositories', to tame fires, explosions or dry wells. Now working as an independent, Max could name his own price and the major oil companies queued up for his services. This assignment was another big one. A major explosion had destroyed the wellhead and a fire was raging out of control. Max had been called by the CEO of PanGlobal Oil to sort out the problem and a private Learjet had whisked him from Houston to Heathrow. After a brief stop to refuel, he was flown to Algiers before transferring to the chartered Cessna. It had been judged far too risky for a jet to attempt a landing at the tiny El Merk airfield, where the surface of the short runway was almost as rough as the surrounding desert.

Desperately tired after his long flight, Max dozed fitfully. When a bad pothole jolted his aching back, he sat up and rubbed his eyes. They were in hilly country now and his watch told him it was mid afternoon.

'Where the Hell are we, Ibrahim? I can't see any signs of the fire yet. What's going on?'

'Actually, we're almost there. You'll be staying in this guest house while you're with us.'

Almost at once, the Humvee turned off the track onto a driveway leading to a group of white buildings surrounding a dusty courtyard. As the 4x4 stopped, the driver and the porter jumped out. They grabbed his bags and carried them into the largest building while Ibrahim escorted him to a large reception area, furnished with expensive-looking rugs, voluminous curtains and a number of low chairs grouped around a large charcoal brazier. It was cool in the house and, with a cold cloudless night to be expected in this arid region, the warm glow was welcome.

'There is a bathroom through that door on the left, Mr. Milton. You may want to freshen up before we talk about the situation here. You will find your bags in the adjoining bedroom.'

Still jet-lagged from his journey, Max was glad to accept the invitation and emerged a few minutes later feeling much better.

'Please do sit down. I have taken the liberty of ordering tea. Unfortunately, we are not able to offer you alcohol in this house but I hope that this will not be a problem for you.'

'That's fine. I guess I can get a scotch or a beer from Chuck Jurgens. And now I've arrived, it's time to call the site for an update.' Max pulled out his cell phone. After a few moments, he looked up, frowning.

'You should have told me. I can't get any sort of signal out here. For God's sake, Ibrahim, how do I contact Chuck's office?'

'Perhaps I may call you Max now and also introduce myself properly. Here's my card.'

Max studied it briefly. In Arabic and French it read:

Ibrahim Falouni
Attachèe de Presse
Groupe Islamique Armeé

Jumping to his feet he shouted. 'What's going on? Why are we here? I demand—' Before he could say more, the burly driver materialised beside him and pushed Max back into his chair.

'Relax, my friend. This situation is part of the fortunes of war – and, believe me, it is a war. But don't worry, you are a uniquely valuable commodity. Like captured Crusaders centuries ago, you will be well treated until you can be re-leased in return for a very large ransom. Until then, you are my honoured guest. I'm sorry you've been kidnapped, but you are free to walk about, read or write. We've already searched your bags, so we know that you are unarmed and no threat to us or our cause.'

Max was shouting. 'I can't believe this. You sit there as though you rule the world telling me I'm a prisoner. And you do that as casually as if... as if you were telling me that my car needs servicing.' He slumped back in his chair, thinking furiously.

It was obvious that this urbane Algerian with his civilised exterior was totally ruthless at heart. He would kill Max in a heartbeat if it suited his cause. The British Government would never allow ransom money to be paid, so his desperate situation demanded a plan of action. After a strained silence, while Ibrahim inspected his nails and consulted a small notebook, Max spoke more calmly, 'Could I at least have my bag from the bedroom? I would like to review my notes – and I could tell you something about my work.'

Ibrahim crossed one immaculately trousered leg over the other. 'But of course. I should be very interested. I'll ask Ahmed to bring your bag. Then he can take your order for our evening meal. There are only four of us here and he's an excellent cook.'

Ibrahim spoke to Ahmed rapidly in Arabic, while the black driver lounged in a chair the other side of the brazier, his eyes never leaving "The Professor". Within a few moments, Ahmed was back and, as Max stood up, dumped the leather bag on his chair.

'So, Max, what would you like for dinner? We have excellent lamb, simply grilled perhaps, or Ahmed's excellent Tagine? Or there is kid, and some duck, I believe.'

'Those are difficult choices, Ibrahim. Just let me have a moment to think, while I look for something in my bag.' Max unzipped it and produced a heavy green sphere the size of a small melon. 'That's what I use to fix problems with oil wells, Ibrahim. Catch!' With that he tossed the ball – but, not to his captor. Instead he lobbed one of his 'Milton's Suppositories' into the charcoal brazier, took a deep breath and dived behind the shelter of the chair. Before the others could react, there was a loud explosion. The whole building shook violently and the floor heaved.

The blast wave threw blazing charcoal embers everywhere, burning everything they touched. Deadly poisonous fumes filled the room as the three terrorists choked and screamed. Max emerged, fished in his bag for the respirator and swiftly strapped it on. Ibrahim was beyond help; the brazier had been blasted into his lap. Ahmed was also dead, felled by a large ember that still glowed in his left eye. The driver would never drive again, his chest speared by a hefty bar from the basket of the exploding brazier.

Max went to the driver, found the Hummer's keys in his pocket and took a Glock automatic from the dead man's shoulder holster. He flinched from the pain in his back as he dragged his fire-resisting leather bag into the bedroom, picked up his computer case, then went through French doors into the courtyard. Nobody was about; there were no more Islamists. He ripped off the respirator, and took a luxurious breath of pure air. Then, holding the Glock at the ready, he painfully dragged his bags to the Humvee. Within a few moments he had found a map in a door pocket and checked the built-in compass. Just as he drove off, there was another explosion from the house, the few remaining windows blew out and flames shot up towards the roof.

After twenty minutes, Max could just make out the smoke from the wellhead fire on the horizon. He started to sing 'Rule Britannia' as the Hummer ate up the miles to the oil drilling site.

❧

Airport Encounter

The departure area is crowded and your plane is delayed. It should be boarding in 30 minutes, so there is time for a quick coffee in Costa and a look at the paper. But it's absolutely essential that you don't miss the flight – the future of the company depends on you, Colin Westerman, to be successful at today's crucial meeting in Dubai. You queue, take your cappuccino and get lucky; a couple leave and you grab the only table in the coffee bar. As you sit down a young man, with a Barista T shirt swoops on the table. He has black hair and a blond moustache; he has a butterfly tattoo on his wrist. Eager to show off his English, he chats merrily as he cleans the table like a whirlwind. 'I am in this fine country seven months now. I love my work. Everyone call me Speedy,' He simpers. 'Have a good trip'. Speedy whisks away the tray of empty cups and discarded napkins and zooms off with the panache of Billy Elliott.

You glance at your watch and frown at your paper. The headlines are as sensational as ever and the stories are mostly rubbish. Your shoulders ache a bit and as you fold the paper, it's a relief to stretch and check your briefcase. As you do, you notice a harassed woman carrying a coffee. She approaches your table, homing in on the vacant seat. Her camel coat is classic and she carries a smart briefcase. A blue scarf complements her fair skin, high cheekbones and piercing blue eyes. At that moment the world tilts and you freeze. Surely it can't be Linda, not after all these years.

The past returns in a dazzling flash. You stop breathing. She sets down her coffee, not even looking up. 'I hope this isn't taken'.

You find it difficult to speak and keep your head down. Your voice comes out as a croak, 'No, that's fine.' Only when she sits down and looks up, do your eyes meet. She gasps and clutches the blue scarf. Colour rises to her cheeks. 'Colin, is it really you – after all these years? What happened, for God's sake?'

From both of you the words pour out in a torrent. You were only eighteen and Linda was two years younger when Linda's father uprooted his family from their smart detached house in an Oxford suburb. Magnus Nordstrom was a Colonel in the American air force, his group relocating to an airbase in Nevada so that he could be part of a logistics team supporting the war in Vietnam. Linda wept as she was led from the house. You were away on an Outward Bound course; your own parents were visiting the Cheltenham Festival, so she scribbled a note and said she would write later. You never got the note; fire destroyed your family home over that same weekend. When the news reached your parents, they raced home, only to suffer a fatal crash near Woodstock. Distraught, you joined the army and moved overseas. This chain of events was the reason that you lost contact with Linda. Without mobile phones or internet, there was no way you could have reached out to each other.

You clasp Linda's hand as the coffee goes cold – but you drain your cups anyway. You tell each other about failed marriages, bereavement, a series of jobs in different cities. Time flies. You beg Linda to meet you again somehow, somewhere. She longs for that happy meeting too – but in a few minutes she has to fly to Mumbai to continue her charity work. As you try to find a way to arrange time together, Colin is dimly aware of the P.A. System – 'this is the final call for passenger Westerman for Emirates flight EK030 to Dubai.'

You leap to your feet. 'Oh God! I really must go now, right now. Look, here's the best way to reach me.' You scribble your email address on a napkin, kiss Linda briefly on the cheek and dash towards the boarding gate.

Linda stands, looking forlornly at your departing figure as you force your way through the crowd. She has moved a few steps away from the table to catch that final glimpse. Her eyes fill with tears. Half blinded, she gropes her way back to her seat and collapses, shoulders shaking. She finds a tissue and tries to dry her eyes. Her makeup has run and she feels wretched, but also elated, now that she has found you again. At least she has your email address. She looks for the napkin, but the hyperactive waiter has already cleared the table and everything has gone. She looks wildly about her – could it have dropped on the floor? No, there is nothing there. She screams at the passing waiter, who stops in his tracks?

'Did you just clear this table? Where is the napkin with the email address? You must have seen it. Please, you've got to help me.'

Speedy stammers. 'I'm sorry lady. I just do my job and my boss makes me clear everything as quick as possible. Cups, cutlery and such in the blue bins and all the other stuff straight down the chute to the big waste bin in basement. So, is all gone. Really sorry lady. Hope is not too important.'

The ballet is missing from the waiter's movements as he clears tables, casting anxious glances back towards Linda. Who has sunk down on the table, her head in her hands, shoulders shaking uncontrollably.

Meanwhile, you are gasping for breath as you collapse into your seat, completely unaware of the situation you left behind. The plane door is slammed shut seconds after you step on board. You relax with a happy smile on your face as the plane taxies for takeoff. The negotiation in Dubai will provide the icing on the cake. Life is going to be really, really wonderful in the future, all thanks to that chance meeting.

Rendezvous

It is a sunny Wednesday, the tranquil interval after the bustle of market day; it is the sleepiest afternoon of the week. Marie Dumont sits on a high stool behind the bar of the Restaurant Lamartine. Once, this place was famous and it still boasts white linen tablecloths, but its dark wall panels and sombre lighting make it gloomy, even when the sun shines. Marie sighs. How she would like to have the money to transform it, to bring it back to its former glory.

She is a widow, but finds it easy to run the bar, with its traditional menu, helped in the evenings by her daughter Annette and one or two extra staff. Hers is a modest but thriving enterprise.

More than two hours ago she served Henri and Paul Leclerc steaming plates of her famous cassoulet, then cheese, with tarte Tatin to follow. They are staying on for their weekly chat when the brothers relax, discussing politics, football, their businesses – a bakery and a small welding workshop – and the state of the world. They also play dominoes, as they have done every Wednesday for almost twenty years – and they are the only customers.

The brothers are sitting in the corner at their usual table. Marie carries over a tray with their coffee, their Pernods and their cognacs.

With her woollen shawl draped around her bony shoulders, Marie knits while she keeps one eye on her customers and the square outside. A fly buzzes insistently, knitting needles click, dominoes clack and the clock on the wall ticks and tocks. There are no other sounds. After a while Marie lays her knitting aside and glances at the mirror. The casual observer would see an ageing woman without much insight on life or the world.

Nothing could be further from the truth. Behind horn-rimmed glasses, the shawl, a pair of nondescript shoes, the dowdy apron and the tired, shapeless clothes, Marie has a sharp mind; she is a keen observer of people and things. Nobody would have guessed that before she married into the restaurant business, she had been a military aircraft designer with Aerospatiale in nearby Toulouse. She takes a sip of red wine and looks at the clock. It is exactly three o'clock.

Through the window she sees the local train from Toulouse pulling into the railway station across the square. Yes, it is right on time as usual. In precisely four minutes, the bar will come alive as the girl in the red beret comes in and takes one of the red banquettes to the side of the bar, as she's done for many weeks. She arrives, taking off her sunglasses and setting her small handbag on the white tablecloth. As soon as she sits down, Marie brings her a Dubonnet and goes back to her perch.

On her previous visits to the bar every Wednesday the girl was usually watchful. She always met a man, a blond giant, who would park his car, an impressive white Peugeot 508, on the square outside. Then he strode into the Restaurant at almost exactly twenty minutes past three. But their behaviour was strange. As they talked the girl's eyes were everywhere. At some point she would surreptitiously pass him a thin envelope; he handed back a bulkier one.

This unusual behaviour suggested to Marie that there could be some blackmail going on. But they seemed to be on good terms; so, blackmail just didn't make sense.

Nor could they be lovers because they didn't stay long,

the man barely having time to finish his drink – he always had a Jack Daniels on the rocks, ordered in an accent that Marie couldn't place – before leaving. Then he drove off, while the girl returned to the station. It was all very strange. Just thinking about it was difficult for Marie Dupont. She admitted to herself that she was baffled.

But today the girl's behaviour is different. Although she wears a jaunty red beret, she seems on edge. She keeps looking at the reflections in the ornate mirrors. Soon she starts to twirl the stem of her empty glass. She grows more jittery as the minutes go by, twisting in her seat and looking towards the square. Then, almost fifteen minutes later than usual, she hears the distant car, then the squeal of tyres. Standing abruptly, she rummages in her bag. Marie sees her wedge a slim envelope behind the cushions of the banquette and drop a ten euro note on the table before moving quickly to the door.

As she opens it she pauses, looks straight into Marie's eyes, then rushes outside towards the white Peugeot as it skids to a stop with three police cars in pursuit.

Men in riot gear leap out and grab the girl as she struggles and screams, losing her beret as she tries to break free, but she is dragged to one of the police Citroens. The blond man has jumped out of the Peugeot. He is shot in the leg as he tries to make a run for it. He shouts in a foreign language as he is dragged into another police car. The two captives are driven off.

Back in the Restaurant the Leclerc brothers are staring out of the window. Soon Marie joins them, but not before she has retrieved the sunglasses and the slim envelope, printed with the Aerospatiale logo, from the banquette. Slipping it open, she sees that it contains nothing but a data disk. She smiles furtively, understanding everything clearly now. With an effort she composes herself and slips the envelope into the pocket of her shapeless apron.

A tall, silver-haired man steps out of the third car. His piercing grey eyes take in the square and the faces at the window of the restaurant. He pushes open the door and wrinkles his aquiline nose. He asks if anyone has seen that woman or her companion before. The Leclerc's look at each other and answer with an indifferent shrug. When he turns to Marie Dumont, her response is equally unhelpful. 'No, Monsieur, I've never seen that young woman in here before today.' The policeman frowns, swears under his breath, storms out of the Restaurant Lamartine, gets into the waiting car and slams the door. After he is driven away, the square becomes somnolent again.

Marie maintains a poker face, caressing the prize in the pocket of her apron. She can see it all now. She has just got hold of a very valuable data disk. It seems certain that the blond man had been buying technical secrets – obviously from Aerospatiale – on behalf of a foreign power. Now, if she is really smart, really, really careful and not too worried about honesty, it can be her turn to make some serious money. At long last it can be Marie Dumont's golden opportunity to get some decent clothes and give this place an expensive modern makeover. She smiles broadly as she has a brilliant idea, one that is sure to bring her luck; she will rename her restaurant *Le Beret Rouge*.

❧

Santa's Train Set

Jim Hardwick was a widower in his late sixties. A twinge of rheumatism made him grunt as he got off the bus in the Market Place. Swathed in an old-fashioned dark blue anorak, weariness seemed to have taken over his body as he clumsily hefted a large duffel bag and picked up an oversized carrier covered in Christmas motifs; reindeer, snowmen, angels and stars. They seemed to hinder him as he shouldered his way into the Ten Hands Café, but it wasn't their weight or bulk. He was just sad, gloomy and depressed. He ordered a cappuccino and stumbled to the back of the Café, sitting down heavily at a table in the corner near to the garden. Jim hated his job. He had just finished another draining, mind-numbing shift as Santa in the Christmas Grotto at Milton Keynes shopping centre.

It really was more than flesh and blood could stand. It wasn't the little kids — they were great, their shining eyes wide with wonder at the magic of Christmastide. But the older ones were a different story.

At around eight years old, many of those little angels turned into monsters, badgering their parents, whingeing non-stop and tormenting their younger brothers and sisters.

Jim wasn't looking forward to Christmas. His only child, a much loved daughter, was living in Australia. So, he would be forced to endure another yuletide in Banbury with his only relatives – a cousin, his horrible wife and two unruly sons. That was the reason for the large carrier bag; it contained the obligatory present for those awful boys.

Jim had spent all of his working life as a teacher. When he retired, just four years ago, he had been the respected principal of a Primary school in a village near Towcester. He missed the chatter of young voices and the smiling faces of those kids. So, this year, he had taken a job as part-time Santa just a bus ride away. It seemed like a good idea at the time, but the bad behaviour of so many of the children was painful for him. It was never like this in his happy days at Pattishall Primary School.

As Jim's cappuccino arrived, a harassed young woman with a young boy of about seven came and sat at the next table. He was a nice kid, but clearly upset and his mother was near to tears.

'I'm really, really sorry David, but I don't think that Father Christmas can bring you much this year. I know it's hard, but since your dad went away...' She paused and looked down for a moment, 'we don't have the money to celebrate Christmas the way we used to.'

'But can I just have the train set please, Mum, please? That's all I really, really wanted...'

The young kid looked very sad and fiddled with the salt and pepper when his mother didn't answer. She listlessly gazed towards the window until a girl brought a cup of coffee and a fizzy drink. Then there was a burst of chatter; two women, both with young children in tow, came in and sat at a table near to the front of the café. David looked up.

'Mum, there's Jack and Matt from my class. Can I go and talk to them please?'

She nodded dumbly and the boy picked up his drink to join the animated group at the table further along the room. When he had gone, the woman closed her eyes and leaned back, resting her head against the wall. After a few moments tears started to ooze from her tightly closed eyelids and she groped blindly in her coat pocket for a tissue.

Jim could stand it no longer. 'Look, my dear, it's none of my business, but I've got a daughter about your age, and I can't bear to see that you're so miserable. If it makes any difference, I'm very unhappy too, lonely and with nobody waiting for me at home. If you want to talk, then I'm willing to listen. Sometimes, telling your troubles to a stranger can help a lot.'

Suppressing a sob, the young woman looked down at her hands as she twisted the tissue. Finally, she looked up and spoke in a low voice. 'You're very kind, but really there's nothing much that anyone can do. It's the old story; my Jerry's left us so that he can live in Daventry with a woman from work and we're going to be on our own for Christmas, with almost no money to live on.

I really don't know what to do. David's such a good boy and he doesn't complain, but he does miss his dad and he tries to help me as much as he can. He brought me a cup of tea in bed this morning.' She turned away and her shoulders heaved soundlessly. Jim nodded and said 'Yes, he really is a very well behaved lad; you should be proud. I couldn't help noticing.' He said nothing more for a moment, then passed her a clean paper serviette from his table. 'Look, here's an idea. Since my wife died I've been on my own and I'm very lonely. I've got an apartment in Alchester Court and I don't get on with the rest of my family; it would be good to stay away from them this Christmas for a change. Why don't you let me cook a turkey for you and young David? I used to be quite a whiz in the kitchen and I'd love to do it again with all the trimmings. We could have a tree too, and all that tinsel and stuff. What do you say?'

The young woman turned to him, smiling through her tears. 'You are so kind,' she murmured, 'and please call me

Jenny. Yes we would love to come – if you really mean it, that is.'

'Of course I do. My name's Jim, by the way – Jim Hardwick. Here's my address and phone number. Come round at about 11 on Christmas morning and I'll have everything ready.' He got up and started to leave.

Jenny put her hand on his sleeve. 'Thank you so much, I'm really so grateful for your kindness.'

Jim turned and pointed to the large carrier bag beside his table. 'Oh, Jenny try to stop young David from looking at that before Christmas morning.' He chuckled. 'We don't want him to stop believing in Father Christmas just yet do we?'

As he shouldered the duffel bag containing his Santa costume, Jim Hardwick was smiling. As he walked jauntily away from the table, there was a spring in his step. He couldn't help himself; without intending to, he began to whistle 'Jingle Bells.'

Jenny peeped in the bag as Jim strode towards the door. There, in the carrier, was the very train set that David had longed for. 'Oh thank you so much Santa, we'll see you soon,' she breathed. Her eyes were shining as she watched Jim Hardwick leave Ten Hands.

෧

Christmas is Covered

It is around 9.30 on a wet chilly morning in late November 2020. At the kitchen table there are the remains of a leisurely breakfast. The bulky Saturday paper demands full attention, but somebody has other ideas. The little girl climbs onto the man's knee and pushes the paper aside.

'Daddy, it's not school today is it?'

'No sweetheart, you're with me today.'

'That's a shame. I do love being with you, but I really like school. I've made loads of friends. Miss Wilson is very kind too and she has nice eyes. I 'spect she's really pretty but we can't tell because her face is covered to prevent Covered. That sounds so silly.'

'I think you mean Covid, Amy.'

'That's a stupid word and I don't like it. Anyway, where's Mummy? Oh, I forgot she has to work again today. She always seems so tired and the other day she was crying when she came home.'

The man holds his daughter close and strokes her fair hair. 'Mummy is very brave and she tries her hardest to make people better, but sometimes she can't do that and it makes her very sad.'

'I hope we can make her happy in time for Christmas. Santa will come won't he? Will his face be covered? That seems so funny.' She giggles. 'We can do the Nativity play, because we don't have to be covered until we're older. Miss Wilson says I can be an angel with wings and everything.

And it will be quite safe 'cos we're all in the same corridor.'

'Actually, it's Cohort, darling.'

'That's another stupid word and I don't like that one either. Will Granny and Grandpa be coming for Christmas as usual? I do hope so, Grandpa's so funny and I like Granny's songs.'

'I'm afraid they won't be able to have Christmas with us this year, Amy. Their house is still in Tier 3.'

'What's that mean, Daddy? It sounds sad, like tears.'

'It's not easy to explain, but we will be able to have lots of chats with them on Zoom, just like we've been doing already. And we can talk to Auntie Fran in Singapore too.'

Amy sighs and snuggles up to her father. 'So, it'll just be you and me and Mummy together, won't it? But that's the best part anyway.

Now let's talk about the things that I'd like for Christmas. Can you help me write a letter to Santa? Please.' She gives him a hug and plants a wet kiss on his cheek.

The paper slides to the floor. He returns Amy's hug and squeezes her hard as he shuts his eyes. Tightly.

The Room At The End Of The Corridor

Only a masochist would choose the Accident and Emergency Department of a large hospital as a destination of choice. Not even at the best of times and definitely, positively, not on a Saturday night. But it isn't my choice. I'm on my way there anyway, the result of my collapse at the end of a sociable private party. The decision has been taken out of my hands. It is with some anxiety that I endure the rather bumpy ride in the not quite up to date ambulance as it trundles the eight miles or so from Towcester to A & E at Northampton General.

The paramedics are wonderful. Tommy is driving, having provided amiable lifting and shifting after my unexpected collapse. He also helped to attach the bewildering array of sticky-backed electrodes for an ECG – reassuring, as it turned out. But it seems my blood pressure is still stubbornly low. His colleague, Marion, travels with me in the passenger section. She is large, self-confident and muscular, radiating reassurance.

Marion is evidently the senior partner and this sympathetic and competent lady is a real pro, exuding care and competence. We chat amiably en route with my rather anxious daughter, Linda, joining in.

A little before midnight we arrive at A & E. Me, on my trolley, gazing mesmerised at a variety of different fluorescent lights and ceiling tiles as we complete our complex journey. First, our little procession visits Reception. It is still relatively early, so the drunks and fighters are few and not yet vocal, though Linda tells me later that her party clothes attract some ogling. We then call at Triage to establish that, as a non-drunk, I can have the privilege of a (quietish) room, No 19. This is furthest away from the mayhem expected later, the room at the end of the corridor. Expertly, Marion and Tommy transfer me sideways from their own ambulance trolley to the all-singing, all-dancing hospital model. Then, it's a friendly goodbye as they leave for their next assignment; I'm sorry to see them go.

Now my care is taken over by Helen, who appears with her clipboard and a sunny smile to put Linda and me at ease. 'Hello, Mr. Hudson. We'll sort you out quite soon. May I call you Arthur?' I nod and smile. Helen consults the clipboard and puts a cuff on my arm. My blood pressure, still low, is tut-tutted over; a cannula is inserted in the back of my hand and a drip is connected to correct dehydration. A blood sample is taken for tests. Helen announces cheerfully, 'a doctor will see you quite soon, darling'. Actually, we expect it to be a long time before anyone appears, as the prelude to an even longer night. While we wait, Linda and I chat about this evening's events. My grown up daughter has had a long career in publishing and is a serious wordsmith, while I'm an aspiring writer; we share a passion for the English language and a sense of the ridiculous. As I'm actually feeling quite perky, we decide that tonight's experience could inspire a paragraph or two. So, we make a start by surveying Room 19, imagining how it might be described in a hotel brochure:

This spacious, modern, uncluttered room has hygienic plastic flooring. A large window with Venetian blinds commands a view of parked cars, marshalled in front of a lowering range of nearby conifers.

The state-of-the-art bed is fully mobile and has a variety of tilting options, combined with infinitely variable height adjustment. For the comfort of guests, the sterile mattress provides firm, unyielding support. Alongside, a comprehensive command/control panel features multiple power points, limited lighting adjustment, call facilities and a powerful suction unit for added convenience.

Two stackable plastic chairs provide uncomfortable seating for guests.

A modern washbasin with mixer taps is a prominent feature.

The suite has the added benefit of disposable multi-purpose compressed fibre bowls. On request, bottles or pans made of similar material can be provided for the convenience of male and female guests.

It is now approaching 1.30am. As we mull over our virtual brochure, another nurse appears. She is called Emma and also carries a clipboard.

'Has the doctor seen you yet, Arthur?' She enquires brightly.

'No, not yet.'

'Oh, that's strange. The display in the office said that the doctor was imminent. I'll be back again soon.'

Emma disappears as suddenly as she arrived. Linda and I crack up. 'It seems that Doctor Imminent has been delayed,' we chuckle. We warm to our theme – 'Perhaps Doctor Imminent is being assisted by Doctor Presently.' Followed a little later by, 'The two doctors have called for extra assistance from Nurse Waitabit.' Our conversation drifts back to writing and books. As we are talking about that extraordinary phenomenon, 'Fifty Shades of Grey', we are interrupted by another nurse. She is a breezy and intelligent lady called Sarah.

'Were you talking about 'Fifty Shades of Grey'?' She enquires.

'Well, yes, but neither of us has read it.'

'I have and so has my sister – we both think it's repetitive rubbish, but we're getting the other two as well.' She giggles. 'It's really very rude indeed.'

Sarah takes my blood pressure again. It has recovered a bit, but is still too low for comfort. While she takes the readings we talk about books; she seems to enjoy many of the same authors as Linda and me. While Sarah notes my readings I mention that I've written a book. The reaction is surprising.

'What, you're an actual author? Wait till I tell my sister! What's your book about – is it a novel?'

I give her a condensed sales pitch. Even in my fragile state, the marketing reflex kicks in; I rummage in my trouser pocket and find her a crumpled leaflet. Sarah has a quick look at the flyer.

'Right. Wow! That looks very interesting. I'll go onto Amazon as soon as I get home.'

In another moment she has gone, proudly bearing her clipboard and its significant readings back to the base of operations near Reception.

Linda and I chat about the enthusiastic nurse who reads so much. What is her life like away from the hospital, we wonder.

All the medical staff must have fascinating back stories of their own – meat and drink for writers. We decide to pay better attention.

It is now around two in the morning; there is a growing awareness that it's a long time since I had a trip to the loo but I am immobilised by my attachment to the saline drip. The red call button on the end of a long cable is duly pressed. A few moments later a different nurse appears.

'Hello, darling, my name's Rachel. What's the problem?' I explain and she nips out, quickly returning with one of the primitive, utilitarian, compressed fibre bottles.

Linda stands up and asks for directions to the Ladies' loos, whispering, 'You can have your pee in private now,' as she leaves with Rachel.

As I enjoy the blessed relief, the noise levels outside increase sharply. It sounds as though this night's crop of battered, mostly intoxicated patients has started to arrive in earnest.

I carefully park my well-filled bottle for collection later. After ten minutes or so the noise outside escalates and there are a few wolf whistles; a few moments later, Linda comes in rather quickly, looking slightly pink.

'My God,' she says breathlessly, 'Talk about running the gauntlet – it's like Hell on wheels out there.'

I'm about to commiserate when I realise that she is holding back an explosion of laughter. 'I've just got to tell you, Dad, these A & E people are so funny. I really don't know how they can keep their sense of humour when they have to deal with all these drink-sodden morons. Just listen.

'Well, I went in search of the loos, only to be told that the ones nearby were all out of order. That nice nurse Sarah said I should go back to Reception and they would show me some others. She also asked me to give a message to Nicky on the desk. I was to ask her to stop looking out of the window and get on with some work.

'When I found Nicky, she was frantic. The phone wouldn't stop ringing, she was up to her eyes in paperwork, where she frantically searched for something vital. Cold scum had formed on an untouched cup of coffee by her elbow.

'Having grabbed her attention long enough to get

directions to the loo, I delivered Sarah's message. Nicky didn't bat an eyelid. "Please tell Sarah that I'm far too tired to do any work just now and I'm probably going to skive off to the canteen soon." Dad, she said that without looking up and never missed a beat in her paperchase. Wasn't that hilarious?'

I laughed along with Linda and asked about the mayhem outside.

'They're mostly male, drunks of course, but there are a few women too. Some of them are egging on their men to carry on fighting. It's ghastly. I think the staff here all deserve medals.'

There is more shouting, with obscenities added for effect; there are occasional female interjections. We are fed up with the whole thing. There is still no sign of 'Doctor Imminent', so we decide to get some rest if we can. I try to get comfortable on my mattress; it seems to be made of compressed cardboard. Linda does her best to find a way to relax on a pair of ill-matched chairs. Eventually we doze fitfully.

Just after three in the morning, the door opens. We are surprised to see a male in hospital uniform. 'Are you the doctor?' We chorus.

'No, I'm Gavin, one of the nurses. Have you seen a doctor yet?'

'No, not yet.'

'Well, it shouldn't be too long now.'

After offering us drinks – water, quickly provided – Gavin disappears. Realising that people naturally expect nurses to be female and doctors to be male, we talk about gender prototypes. Our philosophical debate is interrupted as the door opens again and 'Doctor Imminent' arrives.

Linda and I avoid eye contact for fear of cracking up. Not only is the doctor, unexpectedly, an elegant woman, but she is also clad in an immaculate Moslem gown and a headscarf of dark cream. Her voice has not a trace of accent; it is beautifully modulated and conveys calm and authority. This lady has presence. She consults a clipboard.

'Please call me Vicky. So, Mr. Hudson, how young are you, exactly?'

I have difficulty speaking normally, but stammer that I am eighty-four next birthday. She gives me a swift, expert examination and consults the clipboard again.

'Well, there's nothing seriously wrong, Arthur – I hope you don't mind if I call you Arthur?' I am charmed and smile my agreement. 'Your blood pressure is improving, but you're dehydrated. We'll keep you on the drip a while longer to correct that. Assuming your blood pressure comes back up to where it should be, then you can go home around breakfast time. OK?'

I nod and thank her. She is gone, leaving slight trace of an exotic perfume. Linda and I have fresh material for our discussion about stereotypes. We doze a bit. Our opportunities for sleep are disturbed. The din from the rabble in Reception has eased off a bit, but close by an elderly woman groans loudly at regular intervals. A man's voice makes soothing noises, but to little effect; sometimes the wretched woman calls querulously for a nurse. The night drags on.

A new nurse, Kelly, appears. She is brisk and matter-of-fact. She is civil enough, but fiddles inexpertly with the cannula in the back of my hand. She seems to be unhappy with its connection to the saline drip. Finally, she goes.

'That should be OK now, Arthur.' She gathers up the clipboard and goes to her next assignment.

Time passes slowly. We hear more comings and goings. Peeping around the door, Linda reports that a young woman lies in a bed in a partially curtained alcove on the other side of the corridor; she appears to be in distress and her ashen face is streaked with tears.

A doctor – male, this time – approaches and Linda retreats. The elderly woman's regular groaning continues. Time drags. Linda goes to search for water again and comes back with two plastic cups. She reports that the hubbub has died down and senses that a new crew is now on duty.

Around 6.30 am another nurse appears. She seems to be a bit more senior than some of her predecessors.

'Good morning, Arthur, I'm Gemma. I'm just going to take your blood pressure again and if it's all looking good, you can go home.'

Gemma is as good as her word. Everything is normal again. So, the saline drip is detached and the cannula is removed from the back of my hand.

After a phone call to summon a taxi and a pitstop in Reception for a much-needed soft drink, we step out into the morning sunshine. The taxi whisks us away from Northampton General.

It will be a long time before either of us will forget our long, interesting night in the room at the end of the corridor.

∂∾

Incident at Badger's Tump

Harry sighed, stuffed the newspaper under his arm and walked out into the shimmering afternoon heat. He neared the ancient Mini in the car park of the *Bull* as three young-sters, evidently students, climbed out, chattering like black-birds. They were late as usual — over twenty minutes. That precious time should have been used to finalise details of their project. It was his plan after all and Harry wasn't happy that it might be wrecked by these lightweights. To add to his annoyance, the *Times* crossword was harder than usual; it had taken him all of eighteen minutes to complete today, as he fumed in the empty bar of the Towcester pub. As the oldest member of the group – and, what's more, taking a masters degree in Pure Mathematics – he saw himself as their natural leader. Marching up to the car, he whacked Brian on the ear with the paper.

'What time d'you call this? We agreed on two thirty and now it's coming up to three o'clock. Where the hell have you been?'

Brian rubbed his ear. 'That hurt, you moron. Just relax, we know you've got everything under control. But if you must know, I needed petrol for the car and Emma had to drop off some things at Stratfords dry cleaners. We didn't think you'd mind.' As he had a technical background, Brian was able to keep the aged Mini more or less roadworthy; he was studying for a degree in Electronic Engineering,

Emma took Harry's arm and planted a kiss on his cheek.

'Don't be cross with me Harry, darling, I really couldn't bear it.' Emma was about to start her final year of Media Studies.

Ignoring her, he turned to Kate, a more serious girl, tipped to get an honours degree in Economics. 'At least you haven't offered any stupid excuse. I'll buy you a drink; the other two can get their own. Come on, let's get started.' He marched off, still seething, back into the deserted room at the back of the building with the others following meekly behind.

Harry ordered another half of Bitter and a Gin and Tonic for Kate. Brian, because he was driving, asked for a ginger beer and bought a glass of white wine for Emma. Harry waited, silent and resentful, until the landlord had brought their drinks. Retreating behind the bar, he left them in peace for their 'private meeting'.

Emma looked at the plan as Harry took it out of its cardboard cylinder and unrolled it. 'This is going to be such a cool thing to do. He silenced her with a cold stare. 'There's no time for idle chit-chat. Let's get down to the logistics.'

An hour and a half later they had finished two more rounds of drinks, three bags of crisps, a bag of pork scratchings and two small pork pies. Harry was in a much better mood when they shook hands rather formally in the car park. He had finally got the rest of the team to understand the details of his project. They also accepted that the success of the whole scheme depended on precision in everything they did, needing careful timing, well-planned logistics, silence and concealment. Even that scatterbrain Emma had now realised that their mission had to be taken very seriously indeed. Everyone had got at least one specific task and they had all agreed on their roles and his leadership. Brilliant!

As the trio in the mini drove off towards their student flats in Buckingham, Harry retrieved his bike and cycled back towards his parents' place, Manor Farm, just outside Heathencote. It had been inherited by his mother; her family had been part of the local farming community for generations. His father was a professional surveyor, with a thriving business in Milton Keynes. They were away for a few days, having taken their BMW to drive up to Harrogate to visit Harry's elderly aunt.

Opening the big doors to the barn he carefully checked his father's Range Rover. Yes, it had a full tank of diesel and Dad's gear stowed neatly in the back. The keys would be on the hook behind the kitchen door. He was already finding the wait unbearable. Zero hour was midnight, when he would rendezvous with the others at Badger's Tump, a small spinney on a low hill about six miles away.

Harry went into the farm kitchen and found some cold chicken in the fridge. He wolfed down a leg and some ham followed by a large slice of Mum's apple pie. Then he sat at the table, pulled out his work folder and tried to concentrate on his pure maths thesis but he couldn't settle on anything today. Instead, he went for a walk with Rory, their Red Setter, came back at around five thirty, made a mug of strong tea and took it upstairs. In his room, he stretched out on the bed and raised his mug in salute to a picture of the great mathematician Alan Turing, fixed to the wall above his drawing board. Then, setting his alarm to wake him at 10.30, he drifted into a troubled sleep, haunted by images of complex mathematical formulae.

The shrill tones of the alarm roused him and Harry sprang from the bed, sluiced his face in cold water and dressed for his mission dark green trousers, a black sweater and a balaclava. Although it had been so hot today, the clear sky and total absence of wind promised a cold night ahead. Pulling on boots in the cosy kitchen, he shivered a little as he went out into the night air. It was only just dark, so the sidelights of the Range Rover were enough for him to see his way for the cross-country journey along the lanes leading to Badger's Tump.

He arrived about ten minutes early and parked the Range Rover a few yards off the lane, where it was screened by bushes. Harry doused the lights and listened intently; everything was quiet, except for a few night noises; a fox barked in the distance. It was totally dark now and getting progressively colder. He surveyed the area as well as he could in the dim light. There, a little ahead of him was the big field. Everything looked perfect.

Just when he was getting agitated the others were now ten minutes late he heard a car in the distance. The noise got louder and Brian's Mini arrived, steaming alarmingly. He wound down the window. 'Sorry, mate, overheated a bit on the way here.' 'Well at least you did get here in the end. Park over there by the Range Rover and then we can unpack the gear.'

With the gearbox protesting noisily, Brian managed to manoeuvre the Mini alongside and they all got out. 'You're making enough noise to wake half the county,' hissed Brian. 'For God's sake keep quiet.' He was just too late to prevent Emma from slamming the door. 'Oops, sorry, Harry darling.'

Grinding his teeth with fury, Harry stormed over to the Range Rover and opened the tailgate. Controlling himself with difficulty, he managed to speak in a low voice. 'Here's all the kit. We've got small marker posts, lanterns, measuring tapes, laser pointers and, of course, the theodolite. I'll be looking after that. But before we start to unload, gather round the bonnet and we can all look at the plan again before we start. The other three meekly stood beside the car as Harry unrolled the large sheet of drawing paper, placed a stone at each corner to hold it down and switched on a small torch.

Just as he was about to speak, Harry's torch dimmed and went out. Before anyone could say anything, they were aware of a vibration in the air. It steadily increased in volume, sounding like the fluttering of many thousands of wings. At the same time, a faint bluish light flickered across the surface of Harry's plan for a few moments, then raced along a nearby fence before darting away into the field sloping away from them. The four of them stood rooted to the spot as the blue light was joined by a multitude of others, flickering and dancing across the surface of the field. The whirring vibration in the air continued, rising and falling in volume as the lights swept to and fro. Finally, as suddenly as it had begun, the fluttering noise died away, the lights dimmed, except for a final bright blue flash across the surface of Harry's plan. Then darkness and silence returned.

Harry was the only one to speak. 'I think we should all get away from here as quickly as possible,' he croaked, 'Brian, get these girls back to Buckingham right now.' His voice was shaking uncontrollably, but somebody had to take charge. Dumbly, Brian helped the white-faced Kate into the back seat of the Mini. Emma, completely paralysed with fear, was pushed into the front passenger's seat. Brian slammed the door as he started the car noisily and took off in a shower of gravel.

Harry winced, but there was no point in recriminations – not now anyway. He started the Range Rover and drove home in a daze. There would be no sleep for him, or for any of the others that night.

Two days later Harry's parents left Harrogate to return home. In Towcester, they stopped at Waitrose to pick up a few groceries and a copy of the local paper before driving to Manor Farm. His mother put them on the kitchen table. 'Harry, you look a bit peaky dear, I hope you've been eating properly while we've been away.'

But Harry wasn't paying attention. He was mesmerised by a photograph and headline on the front page of the *Northampton Chronicle*:

'New Crop Circles', said the headline. Harry couldn't read the text alongside, but the picture was crystal clear. It showed a perfect geometric design, beaten into the cereal crop. But every detail of the image was identical to the one that he, Harry, had drawn so carefully on his drawing board upstairs. For a second his face was frozen with disbelief, then his eyes glazed over and he shook uncontrollably as his legs gave way. His mother tried to catch him as he fell, but he was already dead when he hit the floor.

❧

Confession

He picks up the carelessly folded pages from his cluttered desk, reads the words with suppressed anger. As he scans the flimsy pages, he groans and runs stubby fingers through his sparse grey hair.

'Dear DI Grant,

'As you see, this confession comes to you from Jason Chilford, the man you suspected, but couldn't charge. You may have some problems explaining this letter to your superiors. It wasn't in an envelope when I put it through the letterbox at Towcester's unmanned police station last night, so it will have been read by at least one of your junior colleagues before arriving on your desk. I can't say I'm sorry for the damage to your reputation and loss of face; you gave me a hard time.

'I will cut to the chase. Yes, I did murder Nigel Hanwood. It wasn't quite the perfect crime, but it was good enough for the purpose. Here's the background, though you know much of this anyway. When I took up a job as a lecturer in Chemistry at the University of Buckingham, my wife Wendy and I had no friends when we moved from Birmingham to Towcester, but were warmly welcomed by our neighbours Nigel Hanwood and his wife Hazel. Although they were both heavy smokers they were delightful company, introducing us to several other couples in Paradise Close and these were happy times – for a while anyway.

'Then my father died a few months after my French mother, leaving me to tidy up his affairs. As his only child, he left me the house in Kingsthorpe where he had run his property maintenance business. After I sold it, some of his lifetime collection of tools and other ancient bits and pieces finished up in a small self-storage unit at Tiffield. The proceeds of the house sale added to the savings in my deposit account at Nationwide.

'Soon afterwards our attempts to have a child finally failed, with a third IVF disappointment. While coming to terms with that, our friends had a tragedy. Hazel Hanwood was killed by a hit and run driver. We all started drinking to drown our sorrows, but Wendy and I finally pulled ourselves together, while Nigel seemed to go downhill and was smoking more heavily than ever. He kept coming round for consolation and I got tired of this. Wendy, though, was sympathetic. When I'm in a forgiving mood I can see that her sympathy might have been the result of frustrated maternal instincts. But my mood was anything but forgiving when I came home unexpectedly one afternoon, after a tutorial had been cancelled. Finding the house empty, I went upstairs to change into gardening clothes. The bedroom door stood open; Nigel was giving my Wendy ample repayment for her sympathy. After a frozen moment of disbelief I started shouting. When the yelling stopped and I'd thrown that bastard out of the house I went back, shoved my sobbing, remorseful wife into the spare room, packed my bags and left without a backward glance.

'I swore revenge on Nigel. He had taken advantage of Wendy's good nature and I would make him pay. A rented flat in Watling Street allowed me to continue at Buckingham University. It also gave me a base to keep watch on the guilty lovers while developing a plan. It was based on Nigel's departure each day for work in Milton Keynes. Every morning he jumped into Wendy's VW Golf and immediately lit a cigarette from his prized Zippo lighter before driving off. Later, Wendy would use Nigel's car – a rather ancient Ford Escort – for her short trip to teach at Silverstone primary school. Meanwhile I emptied my Nationwide account gradually, in irregular amounts, until I had over £350,000 in cash.

'Meanwhile, I had to be patient. Nigel suffered terribly with colds in the winter and my scheme needed his sense of smell to be almost non-existent. Then, last February, my dream came true. One Monday, Nigel didn't go to work, or the next day either. However, on the Wednesday, he stumbled to the car, well muffled up – but he lit his cigarette just the same. So, Wednesday night was the time for me to act.

'Shortly after 2am I arrived at Paradise Close, wearing a dark hoodie. Everything was quiet. Setting down my holdall in the shadow of the VW Golf, I got to work. Soon after Nigel first moved in with Wendy, I found a spare set of her car keys in a coat pocket. Acting on impulse, I had copies made. Then I dropped the originals under the passenger's seat. It was a lucky inspiration. Now, many months later, I could use that copied car key to open the car. First, I placed an open petrol can in the rear footwell, then doused the rear carpets with water from the large container I'd brought. Then I sprinkled the soggy mats with the contents of a tin of calcium carbide that was among my Father's stuff. Closing the car door stealthily, I locked it before topping up the fuel tank from a second petrol can, leaving the fuel flap wide open. The trap was now set.

'On the Thursday morning Nigel would get into the car. His heavy cold would prevent him smelling petrol, or the lethally inflammable acetylene released by the water-soaked calcium carbide. As soon as he operated his Zippo lighter, a massive fireball would secure my revenge.

My only regret was not being able to see the show. I would have to be back in Belle Baulk, shacked up with an athletic Graphic Designer. She was a passionate woman and I laced her nightcap with something to ensure a very sound sleep indeed. So, an ironclad alibi and careful avoidance of CCTV cameras on my foray to Paradise Close should make my plan perfect.

'And it worked! You grilled me for hours, DI Grant, but could prove nothing. I had motive, but forensics had little to go on after the huge exploding fireball had devoured the car. My alibi was solid too and the pressure came off. So, I got my passport back. Now, seven months after the deaths in Paradise Close and I have completed my escape. By the time you read this, I will be somewhere in North Africa. As you will remember, my mother was French so, with the cash from my Nationwide account, francophone places like Morocco and Algeria are safe havens for me. Extradition? Forget it – they don't have extradition treaties with the UK.

'The perfect crime? No, not quite. Wendy was supposed to survive but, sadly, came to the car that morning and was engulfed in the fireball too. That really was a pity; she might have come back to me one day. Still, it was justice of a sort. It does take two to tango.

'So there you have it. Perhaps a dignified early retirement would save your face? Adieu, Inspector,

Jason Chilford.

DI Grant kicks the filing cabinet so violently that it nearly falls over. He nurses his foot, roaring obscenities. When he's calmer, he cries out, 'Oh shit! Nigel and Hazel might still be alive if they hadn't been caught in the act.'

෨

The Camp Follower

One-make car enthusiasts are an odd bunch. Most are fanatical, with few interests beyond their day job and their passion for a particular make of car. A few have a drink problem or another passionate interest, often mechanical, like clock repairing or optical instruments. Even fewer have something less obvious as their other obsession, butterfly collecting or even writing.

The Amilson Motor Club was one of these strangely tribal groups, dedicated to restoring and enjoying open-air motoring in their much-loved vintage cars. disdaining anything remotely modern and barely tolerating the contemporaries of their own tribe's 'proper' machines.

In the nineteen twenties the French government launched an initiative to stimulate their motor industry. Small family cars proliferated and, as a spin-off, a number of small French sports cars appeared, known collectively as 'Voiturettes'. One of the more successful was the Amilson marque. Many Amilsons survived into the twenty-first century. There was a thriving British club with around forty active members. The much larger French club, Les Confréres Amilson, regularly organised non-competitive social rallies in glorious unspoiled French countryside in Provence or other wine growing regions. Their *amis* from the British club and others in Europe were warmly welcomed, along with chums, wives and girlfriends to enhance the social side of things.

It was one of these events last Summer that Henry 'Sprockets' Wilson, attended along with his wife Chris and another couple, Tony and Gloria Rook. At least that was the plan. The four friends had intended to travel together in a Henry's Range Rover towing his treasured 1929 Amilson Y Type securely lashed to a specially adapted trailer. So, back in February, the Wilsons and the Rooks booked at l'Hotel Fleurie in the Burgundy region for the four-day long weekend of the Amilson 'Rencontre Internationale'. But three weeks later Gloria's husband Tony announced that he was gay and went off with their recently discovered gardener to start a horticultural business. So, the compassionate Wilsons took the distraught Gloria under their wing and insisted that she should come along for company and a change of surroundings.

Early morning starts for the immaculate Amilsons were followed by *'Casse Croûte'* at around 11 o'clock, consisting of paté, cheese, cold meat, local bread and specialities and, of course, many bottles of local wine. The days were warm and sunny, Chris and Gloria took it in turns to travel with Henry in his beloved Amilson while the other 'camp follower' could readily hitch a ride with another driver, as many of them were travelling solo. There would be a boozy lunch stop, more driving through unspoiled villages and deep country in the afternoon and eventually a very late dinner, punctuated by tales of disasters mostly overcome. A typical conversation would start, 'Well hi there, 'Sprockets', did I see you stuck by the roadside again? Magneto trouble was it?' Anyway, I saw you fitting your spare, otherwise I'd have stopped to give you a hand'. Gloria was not at all disconcerted by the technical banter, as her Father had owned a garage and she knew a lot about car technology.

The Rally continued in fine weather and after a day or so, Gloria became a regular passenger for Jack Hudson, an antiques dealer by trade. He looked just like George Clooney and danced with her frequently at the discos after each evening's dinner for the Amilson enthusiasts. By now, she had learned enough about this obscure French marque to keep up with all of the specialised chatter and began to enjoy herself. Jack flirted outrageously and she became seriously attracted to this urbane and charming car freak. Gloria confided to her friend that she really fancied the handsome antique dealer. Chris was delighted to know that she had possibly found a new love to heal her heartbreak. For the last night's celebratory dinner the ladies dressed up in stylish outfits and the men were less scruffy than usual. Prizes were dished out and there were interminable speeches in French. Jack whispered to Gloria, 'Let's slip out into the car park. There's something I've been really wanting to show you.' Chris overheard and slipped her friend a conspiratorial wink.

It was a bright moonlight night and Jack led the way to his Q Type Amilson and stopped. Gloria waited expectantly. Was he about to make her an offer she couldn't refuse? Might he be forceful and relentless? Should she fight him off, respond passionately, or yield gracefully?

A few moments later, she was back in the dining room sobbing into Gloria's ear. 'Men are all useless. I think that Jack's another gay, just like Tony. The bastard said that I was so interested in the mechanical side of cars, he realised that I was someone really special. So I turned to him, closed my eyes and raised my chin. When nothing happened I opened them again. The rotten swine had turned his back on me and was lifting the bonnet of his bloody car. Then he turned on a torch. As it turned out, he only wanted to show off his new carburettor.'

ॐ

Brief Encounter

The meeting ended early and I reached the platform at Euston just as the train was cleared for boarding. I got a table seat next to the window and was setting up my laptop when there was a commotion further down the carriage; a sturdy, dark haired man in his thirties was struggling with bags as he stuffed them into the limited space near the door. I was vaguely aware of him as he sat down heavily in the seat opposite mine. By this time I was concentrating on the spreadsheet that had to be finished in time for the next meeting in Milton Keynes. Out of the corner of my eye I noticed that the two remaining seats had been taken by a young African couple who held hands across the table and spoke softly in a strange language.

The train glided off and the spreadsheet was finished by the time we reached Watford Junction. Shutting the laptop, I was stowing it beside me when the man opposite me caught my eye. I now saw that he wore a dog collar, which came as a surprise; with his muscular frame and plain features he looked more like an athlete – a rugby player perhaps.

He cleared his throat. 'Hello. My name is Henry Masters and I have a parish near Guildford. Are you going far?'

'Only as far as Milton Keynes, for a meeting and then home to Aylesbury. You?'

'Actually, my brother's picking me up at Milton Keynes. I'll be staying with him in a village a few miles up the A5 beyond Towcester. I have to do my stuff in the parish church; St Mary's in Westcote.'

I was getting slightly concerned. Was this man a bi-ble-thumping evangelist? There could be no escape; I was trapped by the African couple, who were still holding hands. Looking out of the window I hoped for divine intervention but the Reverend Henry Masters was talking again. His blue eyes fixed me with their gaze.

'Fact is, I travel around England a lot – to country parishes, mostly. The local people are usually very supportive.'

I gulped. This was getting a bit heavy for my taste and I made a non-committal sound that came out as a strangled 'Oh, really?'

'Yes, and I always make an annual pilgrimage too.'

That sounded even more full-on, but found myself trapped into continuing this embarrassing conversation. 'Canterbury?' I mumbled.

My dog-collared companion looked dazed for a moment, then threw back his head and roared with laughter. Many passengers turned to look – even the African couple. 'Oh dear me no, nothing like that. I go to Memphis, to Graceland, actually; following in the footsteps of the master.'

The relief was overwhelming. There was no fire-breathing preacher. This was an Elvis Presley fanatic! But there was more...

'Oh yes. It's just wonderful. I've been doing my show, 'Blue Suede Shoes' all over the country for more than five years now. The acoustics in these old churches are just wonderful. And I entered the Elvis Lookalike Competition last year and came in the top ten.' He started talking about the clothes, the guitars, droning on and on and on...

It was all so bizarre. I had expected my fellow-traveller to be obsessed with Jesus, but his real obsession was Elvis. We said our goodbyes and parted as we went our separate ways at Milton Keynes. I had to smile when I saw that his pile of baggage included a guitar case boldly proclaiming 'I Ain't Nothin' but a Hound Dog'. I almost laughed out loud to think that this label had been adopted by a passionate young man with a dog collar. Then, I really cracked up; I'd just remembered – Two of Elvis' big hits were 'Turn Your Eyes upon Jesus' and 'Nearer My God to Thee.'

Nothing of Importance

It was the middle of the morning on a warm, breezy Wednesday. Heading down the lane from the top of Frodsby hill, the elderly Vauxhall Astra cruised to a halt less than a hundred yards from the summit. Standing nearly five hundred feet above the river it commands a panoramic view of the Mersey as it runs upstream past Liverpool, then eastwards towards Manchester.

The driver of the old Vauxhall, a smartly dressed olive-skinned young man with a neat beard got out and took in his surroundings. There was a short driveway to Hill Farm and flowering bushes of broom lined the narrow roadway towards the village below. He had already checked the rest of the terrain, with its steep unclimbable approaches to the summit, the plentiful ground cover, several hollows and a few substantial caves, left over from mediaeval mining activity. He zipped up his Parka against the stiff breeze and walked up to the door of the ancient farmhouse, tucked under the lee of the hill.

After three rings, an elderly woman came to the door with a docile old tail-wagging Labrador. He addressed her in his near-perfect English with careful courtesy.

'I'm sorry to disturb you, lady, but is there anyone here who can help me with my car? Unfortunately, it seems to have got an electrical problem and I'm worried that I may not be able to get back to Liverpool.'

'What brings you up here, then – and in the middle of the

week?' Lizzie Foster was suspicious by nature and although her visitor was smart, respectful and seemed harmless enough, she had always been on her guard against strangers.

'I understand that it might seem strange, but it's just that I had an hour or two to spare so I made a trip here with my kite. Some friends told me that this was a really good place for kite flying. You see, many times I used to fly kites in competitions in Afghanistan. I really miss my home country, madam.'

Lizzie relaxed a little. 'I see. What's your name, young man and what brings you to England?'

'My name is Abdul, lady, and I am here to learn tropical medicine in Liverpool. I have only one more year of studies before I qualify.'

After a little hesitation, she smiled. 'Oh well, I suppose you'd better come in and have a cup of tea.'

A few minutes later, Abdul was sitting at the kitchen table with a mug of tea and one of Lizzie's home-made cupcakes. The problem with his car could be fixed quite easily; he had only to coast down the hill to find Frodsby garage at the bottom. Lizzie rang the owner, Fred Abbott, who said he'd just had a cancellation and could look at the Astra straight away. Abdul thanked Lizzie profusely and, while he finished his tea, Lizzie told him a lot. She didn't get many visitors and it was good to have somebody to talk to. He told her all about his family in Afghanistan, raising sheep and goats on a big farm in a remote area. From Lizzie he learned that her husband had died of a heart attack three years ago. Two sons were away working and Charlie, who lived at home, was helping out at a friend's farm in Cheshire until the weekend. Meanwhile, she could manage the chickens, sheep and a small herd of beef cattle on the slopes of the hill. The property had been farmed by her father's family, the Watsons, for over four hundred years.

'Four hundred years, madam. That is impressive. Your family, like mine, has a long farming tradition.' Abdul smiled, revealing brilliantly white teeth. He stood up, shaking her hand. 'You have been very kind to a stranger in your country. You know, you remind me of my auntie, who runs our family farm back at home. Thank you for the tea and that delicious cake.' He flashed another smile, patted the Labrador, and walked out towards the Astra.

Meanwhile in Whitehall Martin Johns, Director of Anti-Terrorism in the northwest, was seriously worried by a series of reports that had come in from a number of sources. It was rumoured that 'something very big was going to happen soon'. Hard information was lacking though; he needed more before getting Cobra involved.

It was 11am on the following Tuesday, a bright, windless day, five days after Abdul's visit when the doorbell rang at Hill Farm. Wiping her hands on her apron, Lizzie answered the door and smiled when she saw her young Afghan visitor shyly offering her a bunch of flowers.

'These are for you. And thank you for recommending the garage. Mr. Abbott was very helpful and changed the car battery; it seems that sudden failure happens sometimes.'

'What lovely manners you have, Abdul. Come in – and let me give you a cup of tea.' Lizzie bustled about, putting the flowers in a vase, filling the kettle and going into the pantry for the cake tin. While she was distracted, the young Afghan looked around the kitchen. Pretending to look at old photographs on the mantelpiece, he cut the telephone line, then gave a thumbs-up signal at the window. A camouflage-clad figure gave a hand signal to someone lower down the hill. When Lizzie came over to her visitor tea and cupcakes, she found herself looking down the barrel of a Tokarev automatic. With a shrill scream she dropped the tray as the Labrador sprang to her defence. Abdul kicked the dog away and before it could recover, shot it in the shoulder. But the Labrador was still attacking him. As it grabbed his leg, he shot it again and this time the dog stayed down. Lizzie had her hands to her face, her eyes filled with tears.

'WOMAN!' he shouted to the cowering woman. 'You are an infidel and I ought to kill you like your dog. But Allah asks us to show mercy, even to those who are unworthy and so, because you were kind to this stranger, because you are a farmer like my people, because you remind me of my auntie and because I like you, I cannot do it. Where can you hide from the soldiers who are coming? Have you a cellar?'

Still speechless, Lizzie pointed towards a door beside the staircase. Abdul fired a third shot at chest height through the door, then opened it and pushed her inside. As he did so, he gave her the key. 'Lock the door from the inside and be quiet', he hissed. 'And afterwards remember to tell your friends about this merciful follower of Allah.' He waited until he heard the key turn in the lock, gathered up the body of the unfortunate Labrador and went outside.

Four khaki-painted Range Rovers had just pulled into the courtyard. A few moments later a large articulated truck followed them, its bulky load covered with a tarpaulin bearing the words 'Farm Machinery Warehouse Ltd.'. A tall man got out of the leading vehicle. Dressed in immaculate battle fatigues, he wore the insignia of a colonel. Another officer, a lieutenant, stood beside him. The Colonel waved his arm and two men positioned themselves to watch the roadway and deter visitors. All the others scrambled out of their vehicles and formed two sections. There were twenty other ranks altogether. As Abdul came out of the farm-house he dropped the body of the dead Labrador into the water trough beside the door. The officer called him over while he spoke to his men. 'My name is Colonel Fadarki and I am in command of this international operation. And, because we have many tongues, we will all speak English on this mission because it is also Allah's will that we should use their hateful language and weapons captured from the infidels to help us to destroy them. He turned towards the young Afghan. 'Your name is Abdul, I think. I heard three shots. You were only supposed to carry out reconnaissance and surveillance. What happened here?'

'Well, Colonel,' stammered Abdul, 'the woman at the farm was suspicious so I cut the telephone line. Then she was frightened and started to run away into the cellar. Her dog came to attack me and I shot it twice – there it is, sir, in the water trough. Then I heard her bolting the cellar door from the inside, so I shot through the door panel and heard her body falling down the steps inside. I also got her mobile phone. Here it is, sir.'

'You exceeded your orders, but, in the circumstances you did well. We will discuss this again after our mission has been accomplished.' He prodded Abdul in the chest. 'You, young man, are not a soldier like the rest of us, but you are also here to serve. So, you will take a bicycle from the big truck and go back down the lane towards the village. At the bend halfway down the hill you will stop and pretend to be fixing the chain. If anyone approaches, you will say that there is a military exercise taking place and you were turned back by soldiers. If that warning does not succeed, then phone me at once on this secure phone'. He handed a small mobile to Abdul, who put it in his pocket, nodded to Colonel Fadarki, turned and trotted over to the truck to collect his bike. When he was out of earshot, the Colonel spoke to his group. 'Sergeant Hakim, order your men to secure the perimeter. Lieutenant Al-Maloura, Sergeant Massoud, Sergeant Abbas come with me into the farm. I will lay out the maps on the table and give you your in-structions.' He turned on his heel and strode towards the farmhouse door.

Abdul was already taking his bike and freewheeling down the hill to the sweeping bend. He had not been pretending to fix the chain for more than five minutes when a middle-aged man with a large terrier on a lead came in sight. As he drew level with Abdul the Afghan spoke to him. 'Excuse me sir, but I've just been turned back by soldiers. They told me that the top of the hill was being used for a military exercise – with live ammunition. I would advise you to turn back.'

The man tugged at the dog's lead. 'That's the second time this year they've closed the hill like this. I shall complain to my MP.' Huffing indignantly, he retreated down the lane towards the village. A few moments later Abdul could just hear the man relaying the message to another walker – a woman's voice answered, grumbling. Eventually their voices faded into the distance.

Meanwhile, Lizzie was overcoming her initial terror as she cowered behind the cellar door, which she had manged to lock. Angry with the deception, she was determined to protect her family's ancient home. Although she guessed that something terrible was going to happen she would do her best to spoil any intruder's plans. She knew every inch of the old vaulted chamber from her childhood days and was not afraid of the dark. Just as she found the torch which was always kept at the top of the steps, she heard voices as the soldiers tramped in to her kitchen. Determined to eavesdrop on their conversation, she stood stock still in the darkness. Although the door was solid, the gaps around it allowed her to hear every word. She strained every nerve to catch their words.

The Colonel was giving instructions. 'As you all know, we have planned this secret mission for more than five years. The greatest care has been taken to ensure total security;

vehicles and personnel have been sourced from many places to avoid detection by our enemies. Success will be rewarded; failure will be punished. We are commanded to make a huge military and propaganda victory today. So here is the detailed plan'

'You, Sergeant Massoud, will be responsible, along with Sergeant Hakim, for the perimeter and the hilltop. You will also distribute rations and arrange other supplies – and you are trained as a medical orderly, I think. So, you will take care of any casualties. Just to be clear, any people – either civilians or from the authorities who approach us will be detained and quietly neutralised. Is that clear? OK, dismissed.' Massoud nodded, saluted smartly and went off to organise his team.

'Sergeant Abbas, you have been specially trained and will be in charge of the Grad missiles. Get your men to collect their heavy equipment and rockets and set up your battery here.' He stabbed at the map with a scarred finger. 'And make sure that you can alter your direction of fire quickly if we need to amend our plans. Is that clear?' 'Yes, Colonel' – and Sergeant Abbas saluted before leaving the kitchen to organise his team.

Lieutenant Al-Maloura looked quizzically at Colonel Fadarki, who had been his instructor at a training camp in northern Iraq. `We will have the most challenging role, Lieutenant. It is no coincidence that we are here on this particular day. Just come along with me to walk our positions and I will explain everything.' The Colonel clapped his subordinate on the shoulder and they walked out of the farmhouse kitchen together.

Lizzie was only hesitant for a moment, but she knew what she had to do. When she was a child and, later as a teenager, she had followed her brothers' example, using the old caves and tunnels down through the sandstone rock to the old-time smugglers' secret entrance behind the bushes in the village churchyard. And all because she wanted to meet her sweetheart, Charlie Foster, without her parents finding out. She remembered those old passages clearly and emerged some ten minutes later to find her friend Sally Hawkins in her village store. Lizzie burst in, wild and smeared with grime, glad to find that there were no other customers. Sally looked up from her accounts.

'Dear God, Lizzie, you look as though you've seen a ghost. What's the matter?'

'Get the police – and quickly,' she gasped, a terrorist group has taken over the hill. Don't look at me like that. Do it *NOW!*'

Sally shrugged and dialled 999. After a few seconds, she handed the phone to Lizzie, who told her story as clearly as she could and gave her location. Finally, she listened to some instructions and put the phone down.

'They said you should close the shop, speak to nobody else and wait for instructions', she said. Sally quickly put out the 'closed' sign and drew the blinds, while Lizzie told her friend more about the intruders. Within three minutes an unmarked police car pulled up outside just as the phone rang. An anonymous voice said, 'Commander Jackson is arriving at any moment. He will take charge of counter terrorist operations in your area.'

Just as Commander Robert Jackson knocked at the door Sally opened it and let him in along with his colleague, Inspector Rachel Nazim. They took in Lizzie's dishevelled appearance; Rachel Nazim helped her to a chair and spoke to her softly. 'You have been very brave. Now you must tell us everything you saw and heard. Nothing is too insignificant.'

While Lizzie carefully struggled to tell every detail of her two encounters, while Sally made tea, trying to be unobtrusive. Very quickly, Commander Jackson held up his hand. 'I'm sorry to interrupt, but this is a very big one. Just wait a moment'. He spoke briefly into a small walkie-talkie. 'Major, I think you should get here at once.' After five tense, silent minutes, an army staff car pulled up outside and Major Colin Sanders of the SAS walked in, grabbed a chair and sat with his two colleagues. After listening to a quick summary of the situation from Commander Jackson. The SAS Major took Lizzie's hands and spoke gently. 'You are a very brave woman. If you help us to outwit these terrorists, many lives will be saved. Can you do that?' Lizzie nodded and murmured, 'Yes of course.'

The three anti-terrorist officers excused themselves and went into the back room of the shop to plan their strategy. Soon they emerged. Commander Jackson. spoke to Lizzie and Sally. 'Ladies, you must on no account make contact with anyone at all. No friends, no family. To all appearances, you have gone off on a trip together. You must stay here until we let you leave. I'm sorry, but it's really necessary.' Lizzie and Sally nodded dumbly.

The British officers realised that intelligence was crucial and Commander Jackson instructed the local police force to carry out house to house enquiries, asking for information about an escaped suspect. Naturally, they were kept in the dark about the real purpose of their enquiries. Meanwhile, Major Saunders called his unit to set up an SAS roadblock at the foot of the hill as cover for 'military exercises' on the hilltop. On another phone, Inspector Nazim was organising a staged crash on the M56 just below Frodsby; this would give credibility for an 'innocent' reconnaissance helicopter, without alerting the intruders on the hilltop. Within ten minutes, the M56 was blocked and a so-called 'police' helicopter had been scrambled to go to the crash site – and return to base after appearing to check out the situation on the motorway. After five minutes above the M56 it flew due South over the hilltop while specialised cameras took thousands of images for the benefit of the counter terrorism team.

Colonel Fadarki scanned the scene of the crash on the M56 with his binoculars and shrugged. Nothing else unusual had happened. He was not surprised when a police helicopter arrived on the scene and seemed to investigate. He felt slight anxiety when the helicopter flew quickly over the hilltop, but all his team had been instructed to keep hidden and the chopper flew South without hesitation.

While this was going on, a British Gas van arrived and a plain clothes team of engineers set up video links. More specialised officers joined them under cover of a suspected gas leak that restricted access to the area around Sally Hawkins' general store. A woman PC was assigned to take care of Lizzie and Sally in the front of the shop; the counter terrorism group was set up in Sally's living quarters and in a large storeroom at the back.

After a few minutes, Commander Jackson came to see the two civilians. 'You ladies deserve to know what's going on. Cobra is meeting as we speak. This incident is receiving the maximum priority and every possible resource is being made available. This is what we know for certain. First, heat seeking cameras have told us that there are around twenty intruders on the hilltop, plus another half way down. There are also four vehicles – two medium sized and one very large. Second, the house to house enquiries have told us that a dark skinned young man with a bicycle stopped a dog walker going up the hill a little while ago. He said that there was a military exercise going on – that's what our own check point is telling civilians too. Third, there are a couple of reports of a large truck with a sign 'Farm Machinery Warehouse Ltd.' going up the hill just before you were attacked, Lizzie.'

'At the moment, we can only guess at the significance of these activities, but the implications are horrifying. We are certain to need help from both of you before this day is over.'

In Whitehall, a grim-faced Martin Johns was facing the Prime Minister, the Defence Secretary and the Home Secretary at a meeting of Cobra. 'Director Johns,' growled the Home Secretary, 'you're responsible for this intelligence failure. How is it possible that a party of some twenty terrorists with five support vehicles carrying Christ knows what, could take over a strategic position in your backyard without your people picking up a whisper?' He slammed his hand on the table and leaned back. The Prime Minister spoke quietly but the words were icy. 'You will have all the resources you need, Director Johns, but what is your plan to resolve this situation?' As he tried to compose an answer, an aide approached and handed him a slip of paper. Martin Johns brightened and looked up. 'We've just decoded an encrypted message sent to an ISIL stronghold in northwest Pakistan. It reads "We have the hilltop and everything is ready. We will give the infidels a deadly blow soon after 1500 hours. Our deadly weapons are being prepared. Allah be praised."' He paused. 'Our top priority is to storm the hilltop before these people can carry out their threat. And to do this with minimum disturbance to the public at large.'

There was a thoughtful silence around the table. The Home Secretary fidgeted nervously. 'Right,' said the Prime Minister, 'not a moment to lose, Director Johns. It's time you got going.' They all stood up and Martin Johns was the first out of the room.

Back in Frodsby, Major Saunders was speaking to Sally and Lizzie. 'You both need to help us. Sally, you will be our eyes and ears in the community. Try to deflect any speculation or rumour and let us know what is being said. Go to the garage, the pub, the post office and make much of the gas leak that has forced you out of your shop.' Sally smiled and nodded. Turning to Lizzie he coaxed her gently. 'We all know that it will be difficult to go back, but you really do need to help the combat team who will have to go through those secret tunnels and storm the hilltop.' Lizzie raised her eyes. 'Of course I'll help. Those bastards killed my faithful Winston and invaded my family's property.'

Meanwhile, Commander Jackson was analysing the scraps of information in the decrypted message to ISIL. The meanings of 'deadly weapons', the timing of '1500 hours' and the very large vehicle had to mean something. But what? As he talked it over with Inspector Nazim. She suddenly looked up, 'I think I've just remembered something. Weren't there protests about a shipment of nuclear waste from Sellafield scheduled to be shipped out of Liverpool? And wasn't it due to happen any time soon?'

'Dear God, Rachel, I think you've got it. Let's follow that thought. Jackson whipped out his phone and searched for shipments of depleted uranium. Within seconds he was scribbling furiously on a notepad. He showed it to Rachel as he called the direct line to Director Johns. 'I think we've identified the principal target sir. A ship carrying depleted uranium from Sellafield is due to sail just before 1500 hours today.' He listened a moment. 'Yes, sir the fact that the terrorists have mentioned that precise time seems to indicate that they have the capability to reach that far. If that's the case, then it can only mean one thing. God knows how, but they've managed to get Russian Grad missiles, presumably captured in Afghanistan. There are much closer targets within closer range too, if they have enough missiles – Liverpool Airport, the Thelwall Viaduct on the M6 motorway, chemical works, the M56 motorway Runcorn railway station and much more.' A long pause indicated that Martin Johns was issuing instructions. 'With respect sir, I don't think that's wise. If we send in helicopter gunships, everyone will know and there will be Hell to pay. And, for all we know, these guys could have ground to air anti-aircraft missiles; how many helicopters are you prepared to lose? Look Sir, we still have exactly 48 minutes before zero hour. I believe we can infiltrate the hilltop perimeter secretly and undetected. If there is shooting, then the locals have all been told that there's a military exercise going on and nobody will be any the wiser. We would have the priceless element of total surprise and we can take them from the rear via the cellars of the farmhouse.'

There was a very long pause. 'Jackson looked at Inspector Nazim as he ended the call, smiling. 'He's given us 35 minutes. If we don't hold the hilltop by then, the helicopters are going in. Let's get cracking.'

Major Saunders was briefed and understood the challenge immediately. A message to his senior sergeant produced 22 heavily armed SAS troopers in the backyard behind the shop. Lizzie and Sally watched the roadway, signalling when the coast was clear. In groups of three or four, the assault team moved towards the thicket at the back of the churchyard. As it was a Tuesday, Sally knew that the vicar would be visiting parishioners in a nearby village. Eight minutes had passed before the assault force, led by Lizzie, entered the cave that joined up with the smugglers' tunnels and the steep climb to the cellars beneath Hilltop Farm.

Colonel Fadarki checked his watch and looked out towards Liverpool docks with his powerful binoculars. Visibility was good and he expected to see the ship carrying nuclear waste emerge into the Mersey in about twenty minutes. His men had done well. Without the means to deploy the usual heavy vehicle to launch the Grad rocket battery, his team of skilled welders had produced a prefab-ricated lightweight platform capable of easy adjustment to elevation and rotation. Six missiles were already loaded and there were twelve more. His rocket team could reload and fire another six within five minutes. After that, he knew there would be a firefight, but he and his group were battle hardened veterans. Just one thing was a little troubling. After the first encounter with a dog walker, Abdul had re-ported no more attempts to travel up the hill – not even the postman. He was about to call Abdul for an update when there was a sudden commotion from the Farmhouse. From the front and back of the building the heavily armed SAS as-sault team burst onto the hilltop, taking the intruders com-pletely by surprise. There was brief hand to hand fighting around the Grad rocket battery, but within five minutes it was all over. Colonel Fadarki had died trying to escape and all the terrorists were accounted for – even Abdul, who had been captured by the troops from the roadblock at the foot of the hill.

After it was all over, Sally and Lizzie sat with Commander Jackson and Inspector Nazir in the general store. He beamed at the two women. 'Ladies, you have been very brave. Sally, your disinformation has worked perfectly. Everyone be-lieves that this was a serious military exercise – with the Gas leak as an additional distraction. Lizzie, you have shown fortitude and determination beyond anything that should be expected of a civilian. A terrible act of destruction and disruption has been stopped in its tracks. We have killed or captured all the terrorists, so that we have seven prisoners to interrogate. The intelligence gathered will be of enormous value. But now I have to ask you to sign the Official Secrets Act.'

'Why must we do that?' chorused Lizzie and Sally.

'I'm very sorry, but this is necessary to protect National

Security. You have to accept that it's impossible to reveal a failure by our sophisticated intelligence systems to detect preparations for this very large-scale attack. You can never, ever, speak of this incident to anyone at all. As far as the locals are concerned, there were some inconvenient military exercises on Frodsby hill. We will always maintain that nothing of importance happened here today.'

Also by Geoffrey Iley

Navegator

ISBN: 978-1782229384

Fast-moving thriller where the work of a brilliant inventor puts his entire family at risk. The action switches from Washington to Mallorca, Monaco, St Petersburg and London as a series of ruthless plans, mix-ups and misunderstandings threaten to turn *Navegator* into cyber-terrorism's ultimate tool.

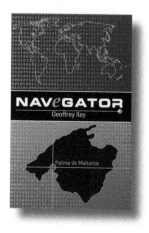

Lightning Source UK Ltd.
Milton Keynes UK
UKHW020934131222
413854UK00009B/121